# THE JAGUAR TRIALS

Photo by Matt Dickinson

Ruth Eastham was born in the north of England and has lived in New Zealand, Australia and Italy. Her award-winning novels, *The Memory Cage*, *The Messenger Bird* and *Arrowhead*, are also published by Scholastic.

If you would like an author visit from Ruth for your school, you are welcome to contact her through her website.

www.rutheastham.com
@RuthEastham1

# RUTH EASTHAM

# THE JAGUAR TRIALS

■ **SCHOLASTIC**

Scholastic Children's Books
An imprint of Scholastic Ltd
Euston House, 24 Eversholt Street, London, NW1 1DB, UK
Registered office: Westfield Road, Southam, Warwickshire, CV47 0RA
SCHOLASTIC and associated logos are trademarks and/or
registered trademarks of Scholastic Inc.
First published in the UK by Scholastic Ltd, 2015

ISBN 978 1407 15504 3

A CIP catalogue record for this book
is available from the British Library.

Printed by CPI Group (UK) Ltd, Croydon, CR0 4YY
Papers used by Scholastic Children's Books are made
from wood grown in sustainable forests.

1 3 5 7 9 10 8 6 4 2

This is a work of fiction. Names, characters, places, incidents
and dialogues are products of the author's imagination or are used
fictitiously. Any resemblance to actual people, living or dead,
events or locales is entirely coincidental.

www.scholastic.co.uk

*for*
*Anna and Elena*
*who showed me the way to El Dorado*

*"Over the Mountains*
*Of the Moon,*
*Down the Valley of the Shadow,*
*Ride, boldly ride,"*
*The shade replied —*
*"If you seek for Eldorado!"*

Edgar Allen Poe (1809–1849)

PROLOGUE

## PART 1 — AMAZONIA

| 1 | THE RIVER | 3 |
| 2 | SABOTAGE | 12 |
| 3 | AMBER AND JADE | 16 |
| 4 | DROWNED GHOSTS | 23 |
| 5 | THE GREEN HELL | 32 |
| 6 | PROFESSOR ERSKINE | 46 |
| 7 | SHAMAN | 54 |

## PART 2 — THE DEATH TRIALS

| 8 | UNQUIET SPIRITS | 67 |
| 9 | DEAD END | 81 |
| 10 | THE TRIAL OF THE HANGING SHROUD | 93 |
| 11 | WOVEN WATER | 102 |
| 12 | THE TRIAL OF THE SAPPHIRE STREAK | 115 |
| 13 | HUNTERS | 121 |
| 14 | MOONLIGHT | 133 |
| 15 | ESCAPE | 139 |
| 16 | WHISPERS | 147 |
| 17 | THE TRIAL OF THE HOWLING HEIGHTS | 157 |
| 18 | FOOL'S GOLD | 163 |
| 19 | VALLEY OF SHADOWS | 170 |
| 20 | GUARDIANS OF THE DEAD | 179 |
| 21 | JOURNEY'S END | 185 |

# PART 3 — CITY OF Z

| | | |
|---|---|---|
| 22 | DEAD CITY | 195 |
| 23 | MASKS | 201 |
| 24 | THE ONE | 206 |
| 25 | THE GOLDEN MAN | 210 |
| 26 | FLOOD | 212 |
| 27 | REDEMPTION | 217 |
| 28 | EL DORADO | 221 |

*The shaman waits for the candle to burn low, then places the necklace of jaguar claws round his throat. Already he feels himself shifting, changing. He takes a fang in each hand and scratches them down his face, drawing blood.*

*With a quick breath, he blows out the candle and all goes dark.*

*Slowly, slowly, my eyes see.*

*I feel my four feet pad the smooth stone of the broad street. Stone buildings tower round me, blotting out the night sky, then open out into a wide plaza.*

*I stand, tail twitching, tasting the air.*

*El Dorado! The last great refuge. The one place that still remains pure and untouched. Safe from the plunderings of men.*

*The stars become points of light on jade water.*

*I see a boy by a river, and a flurry of yellow butterflies rises up from the jetty as he walks along it. He pauses, looking straight towards me. He does not see me, but I know he feels me. His eyes reflect the green and gold of the river.*

*And finally, hope comes.*

# PART 1

# AMAZONIA

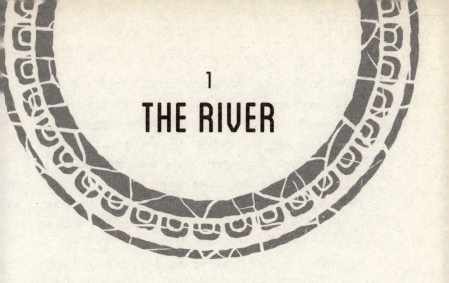

# 1
# THE RIVER

"Ben here, in deepest Brazil. Searching for the lost city of gold!"

Ben stood on the deck, filming the jade-green water across to the riverbank. He still couldn't believe he was really here. The Amazon! A few weeks into the research expedition with his dad. It was the trip of a lifetime.

Sunlight glinted off the dense line of trees. Ben zoomed out; he was using the video camera on his phone. "Here's our fine vessel. A wooden cruiser. Only fifteen metres long. Bit on the *old* side. Been doing a bit of trading on the way. Got some cargo loaded last night – captain won't tell us what!"

Light sparked off the water. A shoal of silver-backed fish broke the surface, then slipped back into the depths.

"Poisonous snakes in there." Rafael was by Ben's shoulder. "Electric eels and piranhas, too," he added nervously, adjusting the bulging fabric of his life jacket. "I read them fishes can eat a whole man in two minutes – right down to the bones!"

"Don't forget them crocodiles," teased Ben, turning the camera on his friend. "Here's Rafael. Give us a wave, Raffie! Portuguese explorer extraordinaire. Expedition expert on all things that can kill you out here. His dad is paying for the trip, so got to treat him right. . . Leech on your neck!"

Rafael gave a gasp and swatted at his throat.

The video shot shook with laughing. "Oh, sorry," said Ben. "It's just a leaf." He gave Rafael a friendly punch on the arm.

"That's not funny," Rafael puffed. He put a hand up to the lens. "Stop filming me. Now! Who's going to watch that thing, anyway?"

Ben shrugged. "Not been able to get a signal since we got so remote, but nine hundred hits and counting last time I looked!"

"Hmph!" said Rafael, but he looked impressed as he bustled off, scribbling in his notebook.

Ben zoomed in on a man wearing tatty shorts and a T-shirt. "Here's the good doctor of archeology himself! Checking the GPS. Could do with a shave. Hi, Dad!"

Dad gave a small salute. "Hello, my one and only son!"

Ben panned to the wheelhouse – but the captain put up a hand and waved him away with a frown. "There's our Brazilian skipper – laughing and joking as usual."

There was the smell of smoke and, as they rounded a bend in the river, a cluster of thatched huts came into view a way along the bank.

"Espírito," called the captain gruffly from the wheelhouse. "Last village for fifty kilometres."

"Getting some good shots?" Dad clamped a hand on Ben's arm and gave it a squeeze. "This is the life, eh? On the trail of the real El Dorado."

Ben stopped filming and grinned. "Think we'll really find it?"

"We're on to something, son." Ben felt his heart thud, catching Dad's excitement. "What with the aerial photos, and the new lead I got from that museum in Rio de Janeiro. . ." Dad's eyes glittered. "I think this could be it!"

Ben smiled. He'd not seen his dad this happy in ages. "Hey, maybe we'll find the tons of gold Rafael's dad is after! Beat everyone else to it!"

"*El Dorado!*" Dad breathed. "But I'm not here for the gold, Ben."

"OK, right!"

"No, seriously. It's knowledge I want to find. To understand how the local people lived. Get the place protected. Preserved for future generations."

Ben nodded. He looked over at Rafael, still scribbling in his notebook under the awning. "But when are you going to tell Raffie's banker dad we're off his route?"

"Yeah." Dad looked uncomfortable. "We're due an update call any time from our Senhor Santa Lucia."

The boat gave a lurch, and there was a wave of curses from the wheelhouse.

"O . . . K," said Dad. "Looks like we're stuck on another sandbar."

There was a grating roar as the captain revved the engine

backwards, forwards, churning up mud and silt as he tried to get the boat free.

"Do the emergency canoes have enough supplies in them?" called Rafael worriedly, fiddling with the straps of his life jacket.

"Don't worry, Raffie," Dad reassured him. "That's all taken care of."

There were shouts, and a group of small children ran along the riverbank ahead, laughing and waving. A fallen tree jutted out of the water; Ben saw a girl balance expertly on a branch. She was about his age, with black hair to her shoulders. She had a band of red paint across her forehead, and swirling black lines along one side of her face. The girl ran effortlessly along the branch and dived into the water.

Next moment she was on the surface again, swimming to the boat with gliding strokes. She shouted something to the other children, and there was a flurry of movement as they jumped into the water and swam behind her in a giggling shoal.

Ben got filming again. "Captain's feeble attempts to free the boat failed. Locals coming to help."

"But what about the piranhas?" fretted Rafael.

Ben saw his dad watching in amusement.

Dozens of small hands pushed at the side of the boat, helping the growling engine.

There was an explosive cheer as the hull came free, and as the boat gathered speed the kids came in pursuit.

"Thank you! Thank you!" called Ben, waving.

"You are welcome!" the girl called back in English.

"But keep to the left!" she shouted as she fell further behind. "The right branch leads to rapids!" Ben could hardly hear her now as the river curved again. "Drowned ghosts!"

He lost sight of her.

Rafael unrolled a map and started peering at it. "What did she mean about *rapids*?" His voice was twangy with stress. "There shouldn't be rapids on our route!"

Ben and his dad exchanged looks. "Just a little change of plan, Rafael," said Dad soothingly. "I'm going to tell your dad all about it when we next talk."

"But white water is totally *lethal*!" cried Rafael. "If you fall out and get stuck in the bottom of a waterfall, you'll go round and round under water till you drown. That's if you don't get your skull smashed open on a rock first!"

"We're going to avoid the rapids," said Dad. "The left branch of the river is completely safe."

"I'm going to check with the captain," said Rafael, clutching the map against his life jacket. "My pa will not be happy!"

As if on cue, the phone's shrill ring cut through the air. Dad fished a bulky satellite phone from a pocket. "Yes. Senhor Santa Lucia. How are you, Senhor?"

"WHERE ARE YOU, MANSELL? WHAT PROGRESS HAVE YOU MADE?" Ben couldn't help but hear the barking voice on the other end of the line, despite the noises in the background – it sounded as if Rafael's dad was in a football stadium.

"We made a slight detour," replied Dad. "And—"

"WHERE ARE YOU?" the voice shouted again. "Come on, referee! You blind? OUR AGREEMENT WAS THAT YOU FOLLOW THE MAP, MANSELL!"

"Well, we're not exactly on the route," said Dad calmly. "We've taken an interesting small deviation to the east, where—"

"WHAT?!"

"Well, as I explained earlier, Senhor, I'm concerned about the authenticity of the map you gave me, and if we widen our search area—"

"THAT MAP IS AUTHENTIC!"

"Well, with respect, several key landmarks have proved to be inaccurate, and—"

"GOOOOOOOOAAAAAAAL!"

Dad held the phone away from his ear with a grimace as a loud crackle of cheering poured out.

"YOU FOLLOW – THE – MAP!" went on Senhor Santa Lucia, once the din had subsided. "LANDMARKS CHANGE AFTER FIVE HUNDRED YEARS – IT'S OBVIOUS! CALL YOURSELF AN ARCHEOLOGIST? GET BACK ON TRACK AND CONTACT ME IN TWENTY-FOUR HOURS." The line went dead.

Dad let out a long breath as he put the phone away. He swore, shook his head, then pulled out some maps from a bag and powered up his laptop using his solar battery. "After the fork. . ." Ben heard him mutter. "Eventually rejoin a tributary that will take us back on to the Senhor's route. . ."

"You're kidding, right, Dad?" Ben couldn't believe what

he was hearing. "So we give up – when we're on our way to the right area?"

"He's financing this whole expedition," said Dad, not meeting Ben's eye. "Senhor Santa Lucia could pull the whole project. We can still collect valuable data," he added, sounding unconvinced. "Come back another time and. . ."

*And meanwhile someone will have beaten us to it*, Ben thought. *Found El Dorado before us!* "Where are you going to get the money to pay for another big trip like this, Dad?"

"Just leave it, Ben!" Dad stood there, fiddling with his gold wedding ring, turning it round and round on his finger.

There was a silence – but Ben knew what they were both thinking about. The cost of Mum's treatments. How Dad had spent everything he had trying to save her. He caught a glimpse of mountains, peaks like ridges of sharp teeth, hazy blue in the distance.

Rafael came over. "What did my pa say? He didn't ask to speak to me?"

"Sorry, Rafael, no." Dad shook his head. "He had to end the call."

Ben saw Rafael's face fall. Dad patted him on the shoulder, then paced away across the deck. Rafael wandered off, flopping into the shade of the awning, then started to write in his notebook as though his life depended on it.

Senhor Santa Lucia not bothering to talk to him like that, thought Ben – was it all part of his toughen-up-Rafael plan? Maybe he should go over and say something. . . But Rafael didn't look much in the mood for talking right then.

9

"Drowned ghosts!" Ben heard him mutter at one point. "Mumbo jumbo!"

The boat continued, cutting through the mud-coloured river. The miles passed; time dragged. Ben felt the itch of insect bites on his face and neck. He filmed Dad typing rapidly on his laptop, then zoomed out on to the landscape.

The vegetation was more dense on the banks now; a mat of woven shadows. Vines trailed into the water at the river's edges, pulled by the current into dark strands that made Ben think of human hair. A tree trunk floated past like a drowned body.

"Fork ahead," the captain called gruffly, jabbing a finger forward. He eased the wheel round with the care of someone handling a bomb, and the boat veered left.

Ben watched the water, seeing leaves and branches carried by the current. A strange animal cry sounded from close by, a shriek that tailed off into a long echoing wail.

His shirt was sticky with sweat. The heat and humidity pressed down. A hot wind had started up, and steel-grey storm clouds formed overhead. Ben rested his chin on the shuddering edge of the boat. Even the water seemed agitated. Peaks of white quivered on its surface. Small fists of water hit against the sides of the hull.

He stared at the long straight stretch of water ahead. No sign of the river splitting into two yet; no sign of any rapids. He saw a dead butterfly float past, gold wings fanned out on the water's surface.

Ben narrowed his eyes, and his heartbeat speeded up. There was something in the water just ahead. He craned forward to look. Something was glinting just below the surface – a silver line, approaching fast. *Metal?* Ben shot up. If the propeller went over that. . . "Dad!" he shouted, pointing. "Look!"

But it was already too late.

# 2
# SABOTAGE

The steel cable was already under the hull. There was an awful grating sound, a watery shriek of metal tearing against metal. The deck lurched. Ben saw Rafael knocked off his feet, his notebook spinning into the water. Ben's heart beat wildly as he held on to the side. *The cable wrapping round the propeller blades?* Ben felt the rapid deceleration of the boat. He saw the captain slam the engine into reverse to compensate.

The boat came to a shuddering halt, its engine roaring. Black fumes belched from the back of the boat and poured across the deck. Ben gagged as the acrid smell of overheating oil hit the back of this throat. "Dad!" he gasped. "What's going on?"

Then came an enormous thud from somewhere underneath him, as if something had punched through wood. The deck pitched backwards and Ben slammed to his knees. Loose cargo juddered across the deck. He gave a yell as he saw his phone shoot over the side into the water.

"What's happening?" cried Rafael, scrabbling round for his glasses.

Ben struggled to his feet, tensing his legs against the slanted deck as he made his way to Rafael.

"Going to check the damage!" Dad shouted, and Ben saw him heading for the back of the boat.

Ben reached Rafael, helped him find his glasses – miraculously unbroken – and then got him standing.

"I don't do water!" Rafael gasped, gripping Ben's arm. His fingers dug in painfully and his face was pinched with fright.

"This way!" Ben helped him over to the first of the emergency canoes attached to the side of the boat, and Rafael gripped the edge of it with both hands, trembling in his life jacket. "Stay here!" Ben ordered. "Till we know what's going on."

*And the rapids?* He scanned the water, breathing quickly. *They still hadn't made it to the left branch of the river!*

Ben looked wildly at Dad. Saw he'd made it to the stern and was looking over the back rail, swatting at the thickening smoke, yelling stuff to the captain. "*Propeller shaft's ripped out. . . No way to untangle cable. . . Check engine bay!*"

Ben saw the captain's face drain of colour; then the man grabbed a fire-extinguisher from a hook and disappeared down the cabin steps.

Ben felt sweat trickle down his face.

The revving engine growled and pumped out fumes as the trapped vessel was held stationary in the water. The backward slant of the deck increased.

"We're sinking!" At Rafael's terrified shout, Ben turned to see a layer of brown water swamp the back of the boat.

There was a stretched screech of friction, the tortured creak of straining timber. Ben's body tensed. *Sooner or later*, he thought, *sooner or later something is going to give.*

Then another thought hit him. *All Dad's research down in the hold!* He made his way to the steps that led below deck. Dad had worked for years to gather that info! He had to try and save the most important stuff, while he still had the chance.

Dad had taken the captain's place in the wheelhouse, and was holding grimly to the wheel. "The research!" Ben yelled at him, hurrying down the steps.

"Ben! I forbid you. . ."

He didn't wait to hear the rest; couldn't. The noises echoing in the enclosed space were deafening, hurting Ben's ears. And the smoke was worse down here too. Was the captain still in the engine bay? Coughing, Ben darted down the narrow corridor, past the storage room door and into Dad's cabin.

His mouth went dry. What to take? Dad had never been the most tidy person – in the tilting boat, the room had become a jumble of notebooks, papers and aerial photos. He scrambled around, trying to select, feeling tension building all around him, the boat being stretched to the limit.

He paused. There was another sound now, too. Low and deep, separated out from the surrounding noise of muffled shouts from on deck and buckling metal. He strained to

listen. A kind of rumbling growl, coming from nearby. . .
From the captain's store through the other door?

Ben grabbed a collection of Dad's things – laptop,
papers, books – feeling the floor tilt as he crammed them
into a rucksack. He heard a slam – and when he made for
the door he found that the heavy bed had slid towards it,
jamming it closed.

*No time!* he told himself, as he tried to shift the bed. *Take
the other exit; through the store!*

Ben entered the murky room. The electric lights
flickered and his eyes stung with smoke. There was that
growling sound again. He approached the pile of cargo: a
tower of plastic crates sealed round with ropes; boxes and
baskets poking out from under a tatty green tarpaulin.

The noise got louder, sending a deep shiver up Ben's
spine. Pulse quickening, he edged round the stack: in front
of him was a large, box-shaped something, covered with
the tarpaulin. Ben's fingers curled round the edge of the
material, and he lifted the sheet up.

Underneath were the hard metal bars of a cage. And
inside the cage. . .

Ben stared, trying to believe what he was seeing.

It was a jaguar.

A black jaguar.

# 3

# AMBER AND JADE

A black jaguar.

A strange sensation pulsed through Ben, wiping everything else out, making time seem to slow and stop.

He put the rucksack down and crouched to look inside the cage, mesmerized, the mayhem round him strangely blotted out in that moment.

He looked at the darkly rippled diamond markings on the creature's head; the way they merged into its coat of sleek fur. *Why is it so still?*

Most incredible of all were its eyes. One was a golden shade of amber, the other a glimmering jade green.

Their eyes locked, and for a moment there was just Ben and the creature; the jaguar and him. Ben felt himself being drawn forward, the space between them closing until all he could see were the green and gold of those unblinking eyes, transfixing him, as if in some secret communication.

"Get away from there!"

Ben was pulled sharply back, his arm twisted so it hurt,

and suddenly the noise returned, the rattling din, and the smoke – and he came back to his senses. The captain's furious face came close, and Ben could smell his sweat and stale breath.

"That's my property!" the man hissed, pulling him away from the cage.

"Dad!" Ben shouted. *What's the captain doing with a rare black jaguar?* "Dad!"

The man squeezed Ben's arm harder. "I already have a buyer for that skin."

Ben struggled to get free. That riverbank post they'd stopped at yesterday – was that where the cage had been loaded on? Had the animal been drugged or something, to keep it quiet? "*Dad!*"

The captain raised a hand to hit him – but Dad was there. He grabbed the man's wrist, face twisted with anger. Then he dropped the captain's arm and pushed him away. "We've not got time for this! We have—" Dad stopped. He'd seen inside the cage. Ben saw him gaze at the jaguar in disbelief for a few seconds.

"We need to get it on deck!" insisted Ben, pulling at the bars to try and move the cage. The animal would suffocate down here if the smoke got any worse.

Dad shook his head rapidly. "No way, Ben. We really haven't got time to—"

"Dad, *please!*" Ben pulled the cage harder. There was no way he was leaving the jaguar here!

And now the captain too was stubbornly pulling at the cage, cursing as he tugged it towards the door.

Frowning, Dad helped, and the three of them wrestled the cage across the floor to the base of the steps, then began inching it up.

The jaguar was on its haunches now, watching them, eyes glinting, fangs bared.

They broke out on to the deck, then lugged the cage across towards Rafael and the canoe; Ben's heart hammered when he saw how much the deck was tilting backwards, how much deeper the muddy water was over the stern.

With each step he felt the vibrations intensify, heard the noise of the engine rise in pitch.

"Lift higher! *Gently!*" shouted Dad to the captain, and Ben's muscles strained as they heaved the cage into the canoe.

At that moment something came crashing out through the deck of the boat, just a few metres from where they were, punching through the wooden flooring like a missile from a launcher.

A chunk of metal.

The captain was knocked off his feet; he landed heavily, and lay there clutching his ankle. "The engine casing," he wheezed.

There was the thick smell of smouldering engine oil, and Ben shouted out as he saw fizzing liquid spray from the mangled flooring. Then . . . *WHUMP!* The boiling oil caught light. Ben gaped as orange-green flames leapt up the stern and licked towards the wheelhouse.

The captain was still down. There was a note of panic in his voice. "If the fire reaches the fuel tank—"

"Boys!" Dad shouted, grabbing a fire-extinguisher. "In the canoe. *Now!*"

Ben helped Rafael climb on board and gave his life jacket a shove. "Sit down!"

"We're going to explode!" Rafael scrambled back from the cage and drew his knees up to his chin. "You can't have that in the canoe with us!" he wheezed. "It's a wild animal!"

Ben saw a jet of foam spit from the extinguisher, then fizzle into nothing; Dad threw it down in disgust. A line of fire sprang up along the deck between them.

Ben felt the heat of the flames on his face. "Dad!" he coughed, smoke stabbing the back of his throat.

Dad pointed a finger at a hook of metal that held the pulley system and its ropes. "Release your canoe with that clasp!" He hoisted the captain's arm round his shoulder as the wall of flame rose. "We'll take the other canoe. Use the paddles! Keep to the left river! Stay left!" Dad's voice was loud above the hiss of flames and the splash of water, and Ben saw the deep frown lines across his forehead. "Release your canoe *now!*"

"Please get off the boat, Dad!"

"It's getting hot, Ben," wailed Rafael. "Very, very hot."

Desperately Ben leaned forward to grab the metal clasp.

"If we get separated," shouted Dad as he helped the captain across the deck, "fire the flare. I'll find you."

"Please be OK, Dad!"

"*I'll find you, Ben!*" Dad hollered as the heat intensified.

Ben unclipped his canoe. He felt himself plunge downwards. Heard Rafael scream. The canoe slammed on to the river and a wall of water rose up, drenching them. Ben was thrown against Rafael, and the two struggled to sit back up, gripping the sides in the violent rocking. Ben saw the jaguar, crouched and baring its teeth.

He felt the current catch under them, the distance between them and the boat immediately increasing as the lighter canoe was caught in the swift water.

Ben rubbed water from his eyes, desperately looking back. He saw Dad helping the captain to the second canoe. Then smoke billowed across them and the black plumes blotted them both out.

"We're moving to the right!"

Rafael's cries kicked Ben into action. He grabbed a paddle and craned forward. He could see the river branching just a couple of hundred metres from where they were – and the space was closing fast. A strange mist lingered over the river to the right, hanging in the air like a shroud. Ben shoved the second paddle into Rafael's trembling hands. "Help me!" He drove his own paddle into the water. "On the right side to pull us left!"

Rafael jabbed manically at the water.

The current tugged faster as they approached the fork. The jaguar paced about in the cage, snarling, and Ben heard the rumble of the rapids drown out the crackling of fire behind him. The canoe pitched over the choppy surface.

"Look out!" screamed Rafael. Out of nowhere ahead of them loomed a rock.

Ben gripped the paddle and dug in hard, cutting a sheer diagonal, only just managing to take the canoe safely past.

*We're still going right!* Ben clenched his teeth and dug in harder. Rafael continued his clumsy strokes. "*Come on!*"

*Dad! Has he got to the other canoe?* Ben wanted to look back and check, but he couldn't afford to. The muscles in his arm strained as his paddle fought the flow, as he channelled all his energy into the blade.

*Come on! Come on!* The canoe made a diagonal cut to the left, veering away from the fog at the top of the rapids, but the current was getting stronger by the second, dragging them relentlessly the way they mustn't go. Ben's ears filled with sound: the boom of water, Rafael's whimpering moans, the crazed snarls of the jaguar. The point of the canoe wobbled like a compass needle.

Then started to swing right.

Ben's body tensed. The river surged forward, the dark slicks thinning into foamy white. He felt the force of the water overwhelming the canoe – but he continued to paddle. He saw Rafael's eyes huge behind his glasses.

*We've missed the left fork. We've missed the left fork!*

As they skewed sideways he briefly saw behind them. Through the smoke and the spray there was a blur of movement. Two figures. He saw the burning boat hit the rock; the two men were wrenched apart; one of them – his dad? The captain? Which was it? – jumped into the water.

There was a line of orange-green flames. . .

A jet of fire as the fuel tank exploded.

*Dad!* Ben heard the word in his head, but no sound came. He covered his face as the heat from the blast hit.

Bits of boat rained down like shrapnel: twisted metal,

charred fragments of smoking wood which hissed on the speeding water. Falling embers singed holes in Ben's shirt.

When Ben looked again, all he could see was the skeleton of the boat, collapsing into itself, burning, sinking.

And Dad was gone.

# 4
# DROWNED GHOSTS

The canoe sped on. Ben saw a dark blur as the jaguar hit itself against the bars of the cage; he felt the cool damp as they went through the fog at the brink of the rapids.

*Dad. Dad.*

Numb, he felt water smack the edge of the canoe; saw rocks ahead, approaching fast, water breaking over them in a churning white crust.

A low growl cut through the sound of thundering water, bringing Ben back to his senses. The jaguar was strangely still, crouched and watching; fixing him with its wild-eyed stare.

And then the rapids were upon them.

No time to think. No other choice.

*Try.*

*Something.*

*Anything.*

Ben forced his paddle into the foam, sending the canoe

into a zigzag, avoiding a rock, then another. Waves slapped his face and went into his eyes, and he had to blink hard to see what was coming. His saturated clothes clung to him like a slimy skin.

Adrenalin pumping, he stabbed down with the paddle, trying to use it to steer, aiming for the narrow channels between the rocks, willing the canoe towards the gaps. Instinct kicked in as he forced the hull into a diagonal swing. "Help me!" he yelled, water gritty on his tongue – but Rafael kept his hands clamped to the canoe edge, gaping at the frothing water.

Panting, Ben braced himself for the next slam as they were spun and smashed. *What next?*

The canoe blade glanced off a boulder and Ben felt the length of his arm jar as the paddle was almost wrenched from him.

His aching body shuddered. *No time to look back!* He plunged the paddle down, his muscles tightening painfully. He crammed all his energy into each stroke. He fought the chaos. He fought the noise. He fought the blinding spray.

The canoe crashed against a rock, cleaving a strip off the hull. The vessel veered, and Ben fought to get control and to avoid the added hazards: thick, sharp branches, rolling logs; a cauldron of debris.

Without warning, the canoe slanted forward, snatching Ben's breath away. They shunted downwards, pitching metres down a waterfall. There was a rebound as the canoe hit the plunge pool, its front lifting.

Ben saw the jaguar cage start to tip and he flung

himself down, grabbing at the bars, managing to slow its momentum. It wedged itself against the triangle of the stern, and the canoe slammed down and shot on.

Ben got back into a sitting position, scrabbling round for the paddle. *What now?*

Almost immediately, the canoe curved down the next waterfall. Ben felt his body scrunch as the canoe jolted up, nearly throwing him out.

*How many more falls?*

Water hit Ben from all angles; spray blurred his vision. He gripped the paddle as the canoe tumbled on towards jutting boulders. He shot out the paddle, leaning over the water dangerously far . . . he *had* to steer them past those rocks. *Had to.* He shouted with the effort, his voice blotted out by the crash of the rapids, every bit of him straining as he dug down and sliced.

The rocks streaked past.

*Yes. Yes!*

Ben felt the paddle collide with an unseen stone surface, felt the wood disintegrate, felt himself losing his balance – unable to pivot back. . .

And then, as the nose of the canoe tipped down the next waterfall, he was falling.

Falling. . .

"On your back! Feet facing downstream! Starfish!" he heard Rafael scream – and then Ben hit the water, the current squeezing him from all sides as he rolled and sank, water burning up his nose and into his throat.

Ben flailed about in the spinning current, forcing his

eyes open. He saw whirling strings of bubbles spiralling upwards, the base of the canoe . . . daylight.

*Aim for the light.* He kicked and swam. He felt the air drain from him as he fought upwards, trying to free himself from the twisting water.

*Survive.*

Ben made for the surface against the relentless spiralling pull. With no air left, his body heavy, a muffled thunder hammered through his skull.

Ben broke out from the water, mouth wide – but no air came. He was scooped up by water. Why couldn't he breathe? His heart pounded. He knew he didn't have the energy to kick away from the vortex at the bottom of another waterfall; if he was caught in a plunge pool again, he was as good as dead.

A desperate idea seized him. What had Rafael said? *Starfish?*

As he hit the bottom of the next drop, Ben flung wide his arms and legs, spreading his weight, slamming the water in a kind of belly flop. And instead of being sucked downwards in the whirlpool spin, he stayed on the surface and was washed on, still fighting to breathe; bracing himself for another drop.

But no drop came.

He was at the end of the rapids, skimming over a long stretch of rippling water like a bodyboarder, towards a thin pebble beach.

Trickles of air passed into Ben's suffocated lungs. He hauled himself out of the water and on to the bank, lying on his back on the smooth stones, chest heaving.

Vaguely he saw Rafael, in up to his waist, heaving the canoe to shore, wedging it against the pebbles; its hull smashed up, half-flooded; the jaguar in its cage.

"Ben? You OK, Ben?" Rafael crouched over him, soaked and dishevelled in his bulky orange life jacket, staring anxiously down. "It'll be all right," he reassured. "I read about that. When you're under water too long, a valve in your throat closes off. It'll loosen soon. It'll be all right."

Ben managed to sip more air, but it was minutes before he had enough to speak. "Did – you – see – Dad?" His voice rose to a shout as more air filtered down his windpipe. "*Dad!*" He broke into a spasm of coughing.

Rafael shook his head. He fiddled with his glasses, the lenses still flecked with drops. "No. Not yet. . . But no bones broken, no – that's a miracle! You saved us! I did good to push the canoe to the side, didn't I, yes?"

"Your idea saved me." Ben weakly patted his friend's shoulder. "Thanks, Raffie." He sat up, panting, and scanned the river. *Where is he?* "If Dad escaped, he'd have been swept the same way as us, wouldn't he?" Ben stumbled to his feet in his saturated clothes, scrutinizing the stretch of waterfalls to the top of the rapids.

"I think so," said Rafael slowly, not sounding at all sure.

*How far have we come?* thought Ben. *A few hundred metres? A kilometre?* He took a few steps along the pebble bar.

*Has Dad survived?* Ben's thoughts buzzed with terrible scenarios. Skull smashed on the rocks. Caught in the plunge pool of a waterfall. . .

He dug his nails into his palm. Dad was alive; he had to believe it. Had to.

Ben made for the bottom of the rapids. Dad might be stranded somewhere, injured, clinging to a rock in the middle of the river. Debris floated past. Something red like blood. Dad's red laptop case! Ben broke into a faltering run. *Get back up the edge of the rapids*, he told himself. *Check the site of the boat accident.*

He came nearer to the bottom plunge pool, breathing fast. He felt the spray coat his face, the air vibrating from the churning currents, the force of it stopping him from going closer. He placed a foot on the wet surface of tumbled rocks that made up the bank – and immediately his boot slipped backwards. He tried again, but his foot slammed down painfully. There was just no friction, no footholds. And further up it got no better. He felt a wave of nausea. All he could see were cliffs and vertical mud, knotted roots over raging water. *How did we ever survive that?*

"*Dad!*"

"Maybe people from that Espírito village saw the smoke," Rafael shouted over the noise of the water. "They'll come and help. They will, won't they? Do you think someone will come?"

"That village was miles back." Ben scanned up the falls again, trying to make out shapes in the fog of the rapids. And who else knew they were here? The stark reality hit. They were well off-route after Dad's detour. Senhor Santa Lucia hadn't even been told their location.

He tried to clamber towards the boiling rapids again, but

there was just no way to do it. He tried to find a way up the bank into the forest, all the time yelling Dad's name. If only he could trek alongside the river, he told himself. . . But the edges were too sheer, too rocky; the permanent fog in the air coated everything in a treacherous slick sheen; and the forest beyond was an impenetrable screen of interlocking branches and stems.

Ben stood there panting. A sudden need to sit, to lie down, overwhelmed him. He couldn't seem to breathe properly again; a throbbing pain gripped his chest.

"You saved us." Rafael was close to his side, brushing his shoulder. "The jaguar as well."

Ben looked at Rafael, then beyond him at the cage.

*The black jaguar.*

They made their way back along the pebble bar and Ben stared through the bars at the half-crouched animal, its paws submerged in the wet floor of the cage. Its fur bristled with damp; its whiskers were beaded with silver drops. Their eyes locked a second time, and again there was that unknown something passing between them. That powerful, invisible connection.

"If we leave it in the cage," Ben said, "it'll die."

Rafael squirmed fretfully. "Yes, but. . ." He stared around the forest unhappily. "Jaguars are man-eating carnivores, you know. Third biggest cat after a lion and a tiger, and. . ."

Ben looked at the creature, crouched so silently. Sleek velvet black. Muscles along its flank tensed. Completely motionless except for the occasional flick of its tail. Ben swallowed. "I have to open the cage."

Rafael gave a strangled cry of protest.

The animal's eyes held Ben's gaze. Green. Gold.

"Go over there, Raffie." Ben handed his friend two jagged stones from the riverbed. "Keep a distance. If anything happens, jump into the river and throw these. Make a lot of noise."

"Ben!" Rafael's voice rose a pitch as he scrambled to the far side of the beach. "We'll be ripped to pieces and devoured!"

Ben 's breathing speeded up. He examined the cage door. It had three bolts – top, middle, bottom. *Slide them*, he told himself. *Ease open the door. . . Step behind the cage. . .*

*Give it a clear route into the forest.*

Heart racing, he extended one arm, reached out and slid the top bolt.

The big cat blinked.

Ben went for the bottom bolt, having to wiggle it a bit to release it from the orange rust coating the metal.

The jaguar stood up, its flank tensed.

Ben heard Rafael make another strangled sound and then go silent.

Slowly, slowly, Ben eased the final, middle bolt. He took a breath, then swung the door open and moved to one side.

The creature stood in the gaping doorway, head raised, nose sniffing the air.

Ben gazed at it, taking in the jet shine of its fur, the majestic curve of its back. Moisture coating it in tiny pearls.

It all happened so fast – there was no time to react, no time to get away.

The jaguar lunged at him. A front paw lashed out. Ben cried out as he felt the pain, acid-hot on his forearm, as the claws made contact with his skin, as four razor points ripped inwards and downwards.

And the jaguar was gone.

# 5
# THE GREEN HELL

Ben watched the blood run down his arm and drip off his fingers, mesmerized by the bright red that was pouring from the gashes.

"We need to stop the bleeding!" cried Rafael, rushing forward. "You could get a parasite infection. Or gangrene! Then you'll have to have your arm amputated! *Raise the limb*," he recited, as if he was quoting from a medical book. "*Apply pressure. Stem the flow.*" He clamped his hand on to the cuts and hoisted Ben's arm up.

"Aaargh! Careful!"

Ben looked into the dense thicket where the jaguar had disappeared. *I try to help, and that's my payback?*

He shivered, suddenly light-headed, and stumbled a little on the pebbles.

Rafael helped him to sit up, arm still raised. "Your dad said there were emergency supplies in the canoe. Stay there!" he commanded. "Keep your arm up!" He rushed over to the canoe. "Keep pressing!"

*As if I'm going anywhere*, thought Ben. The blood ran over his elbow, soaking into his shirt. He felt the sun, hot on his face; a dizziness. He applied more pressure and watched the blood slowly go more viscous as it clotted.

Rafael came back with a dripping canvas knapsack. And a machete.

"Steady on, Raffie!" grimaced Ben. "My arm doesn't need to be amputated just yet."

"What? No!" Rafael dropped the blade on the pebbles. "These were all the things I found. They were strapped inside the canoe." He rooted round in the bag and pulled out a first-aid kit in a plastic pouch.

"Pass that disinfectant," said Ben. He pulled out a wipe and dabbed at the four slash marks and the congealing blood. "I think you can take your life jacket off now."

"Clean the wounds really well," Rafael told Ben, pulling the jacket over his head. "There's a big danger bacteria will get in." He looked wildly about him, as if a horde of microorganisms were closing in on them right that minute. "Your blood will go bad and then you die."

"Thanks," said Ben through gritted teeth. He may as well have been using neat acid, the way his skin was stinging. He used another wipe. Getting an infection here was no joke, he knew that.

He stared back at the foot of the rapids, feeling sick. Dad was out there somewhere. No medical supplies. And Ben couldn't get to him.

"It's terribly dangerous, the Amazon is," Rafael muttered. He stared fearfully around at the thick forest lining both sides of the riverbank. "Terribly dangerous. And there's not just piranhas, you know. I read a book that said there're anacondas and other kinds of deadly poisonous snake." He swatted the air, agitated. "And an insect that can fly into your eye and blind you, and. . ."

Rafael was really starting to get on Ben's nerves. He pulled a bandage from the plastic pouch. Just his luck to be stuck in the jungle with the world's most paranoid expert on jungle horrors. Ben's hand shook as he tried to rip open the packaging.

Rafael took it from him. "Anyway, what happened back there?" His wet hair stuck up in tufts as he unrolled the fabric. "That cable in the water – what was it? A fishing line?"

Ben shook his head. "It didn't look like any kind of fishing line to me. It looked as if it had been fixed across the water."

"What, *on purpose*?" fretted Rafael. "But who would do something like that?"

"Someone who didn't want boats on that stretch of the river?" suggested Ben.

"Someone who wanted to sabotage our trip!" cried Rafael. "Must have been!"

Ben still felt faint. Rafael started to wind the bandage firmly round the wound, and Ben took sharp breaths as the fabric made contact, blood straight away oozing through the gauze.

"There are poisonous tarantulas in these forests," Rafael went on as he worked. "And vampire bats that can kill you.

And flies that lay their eggs under your skin and then the maggots hatch out and—"

"*Rafael!*"

Ben just had to know that *Dad* wasn't riddled with maggots or getting bitten by vampire bats – that was all that mattered to him at that moment. "If you've nothing helpful to say, just shut it!"

Rafael shut it. He blinked hard behind his glasses and looked at his feet.

*He's just scared*, Ben told himself, suddenly ashamed. He stared into the dense green that hemmed the river. He felt the jungle all round them, like a living, breathing thing.

And something more. . . He couldn't place it. Something nearby – a presence, listening, watching. His spine shivered. There was the flicker of shapes through the heat haze and dappled patches of shadow, momentary, figure-like. . . Then they were gone.

Ben shook himself. *You're losing it*, he told himself. *Focus!*

He flexed his arm experimentally, clenching and unclenching the fingers. It still hurt like mad, but he'd have to cope. They couldn't get upriver to find Dad; what about downriver – raise the alarm? Ben scrambled over to the canoe and inspected its smashed-up hull. Maybe they could fix it somehow, or salvage its timber; strap more wood to it. They had the machete, after all.

They'd reach a trading post or another village or something eventually, wouldn't they? If nothing else, they might be able to get out into the middle of the river and see back up to where the boat had sunk.

*Yeah, right!* a voice inside him scoffed. And what had the captain said? *Last village for fifty kilometres.* He'd been exaggerating, surely. There must be something, someone, some way to get help.

"Look at these." Rafael handed over a head torch and compass he'd found in the knapsack, and Ben slipped them in his pocket. "And this!" Rafael held up a large plastic container. He unscrewed the lid and brought out a thickish cylinder. He read the side of it: "*Parachute rocket flare.*" Rafael waved the cartridge about excitedly. "It says here that you can see these things for fifteen kilometres in the daytime!"

"All right! We'll try," said Ben. "But I want to do it."

"Why can't *I*?" protested Rafael. "Why should you always be the boss?"

"No. *I'm* doing it." Inside Ben was a secret hope. His dad's last words went round in his head. *Fire the flare. I'll find you.*

"I've memorized the instructions," said Rafael. "*Unscrew the red cap. Point upwards, away from body.*"

Ben took the cylinder and gestured to Rafael to stand back. He gripped the flare with his dodgy arm. He'd need his other hand to set the thing off.

"*To fire, pull cord sharply down.*"

A trail of smoke shot from the top of the tube into the air like a firework. There was a slight recoil and Ben felt a stabbing ripple through his wound. He gazed up to watch. The streak of smoke became a bright point of light, like a star. It hung in the air a moment, before slowly making its descent.

"*Height three hundred metres,*" Rafael muttered. "*Duration forty seconds.*" He gazed at the sky, as if expecting his dad to arrive in a helicopter any moment.

The glow faded. Disappeared.

They waited, sat in the shade from overhanging branches as the tropical sun beat down. The air was filled with raucous animal calls. Howler monkeys? Some kind of parrot?

Nothing more.

*But then, what were you expecting?* Ben asked himself. He felt the time ticking, heavy, oppressive. Every minute that went by meant another minute Dad wasn't being helped. He paced about impatiently, wiping sweat off his forehead. "We've got to decide what to do, Rafael. We can't just sit here!"

Rafael folded his arms across his chest. "The books say that you should always stay by the river."

Raffie was right about that, at least, thought Ben. Number-one rule of the survival course they'd all had to take before starting the expedition: never leave the river. So they should check where the river went, right? He stared up as a bright blue bird flew overhead, and he followed its line of flight. They needed to get their bearings – a bird's-eye view. And for that he needed to get higher.

Ben looked around for a suitable tree. He found one with bark that was a mosaic of lichen and moss, with brown ant trails like lines of spilt pepper. Roots hung like leather straps from the branches. "I'm going to see where we are."

Ben grabbed a root with his good arm and pulled himself up.

"A bit more to the left." Rafael called up instructions as Ben climbed the trunk. "Yes, that branch – good! Watch out for deadly snakes!"

Ben went higher, taking it slowly, so as not to put any strain on his cuts. He wouldn't have to climb far, he realized, because they were already on a kind of ridge from where he'd be able to look down the river valley.

The view quickly opened out. Ben saw the river's enormous meandering loops as it continued, misty and glinting; the vast forest stretching away.

But there was something else, not far. He shielded his eyes from the sun, wanting to be sure of what he was seeing. He nearly lost hold of the branch in his excitement.

"There's someone out there!" he shouted down to Rafael. "I can see smoke!"

Further along the river. A column of grey smoke. A campfire! A settlement? They could get help for Dad there, sort out a search party!

"How far?" Rafael shouted up. His voice quivering.

"Very close!" Way closer than Espírito.

Ben took out the compass and plotted the course between them and the smoke. They could short-cut it through the forest. It looked so much faster to do that. They had the machete to make a trail.

*Don't leave the river*, a voice in his head told him. *Stick to the river*. But he ignored it. They had to get help. This was their best option, he was sure.

Ben climbed down the tree and told Rafael his idea.

"Are you really certain? We should stay by the water,

shouldn't we? And your arm, Ben! How are you going to use the machete? I can help, but—"

"I can use my left arm," Ben told him.

"Hmmm." Rafael stared round them with a slow nod. "And the people that put the steel-wire could come and get us if we stay here!" He looked terrified at the thought.

Ben pulled at the knapsack. "What else is in here?"

Rafael dug around again and produced a bottle of water. "That's everything."

"But there should be high-calorie bars!" said Ben. "And all sorts of packs of dry food. My dad was discussing the emergency supplies with the captain before we set off!"

"The captain took them? Who knows?"

OK. So they had no food. Ben screwed the top off the bottle. "I say we drink this water now, then fill the bottle from the river to take with us."

Rafael looked shocked. "But think about the *bacteria*," he mouthed. "Think what might have died in that water. I mean. . ." – he corrected himself quickly, not meeting Ben's eyes – "er . . . *gone to the toilet* in the water. In any case," he continued, "you said the smoke is really close. We can drink that now, and have more when we get there."

They shared all the water between them; then, guided by the compass, Ben hacked his way in the direction of the smoke, Rafael following with the knapsack. The machete sliced easily through the wispy branches that screened the way, and Ben felt himself get into his stride. They'd find help. Get a search party organized for Dad. The thought injected him with sharp little doses of hope.

They walked through cool groves where the trunks looked as if they were wrapped round with green felt. They walked down gently sloping banks, bearded with ferns; above them, an overlapping mat of feathery leaves.

Quickly, though, the forest became more dense. Branches snapped back at them like whips; their clothes snagged on thorns and sharp leaves. Insects swarmed round Ben as he cut the trail, biting his skin, leaving tiny pockmarks of blood.

"Don't scratch them spots!" warned Rafael. "Won't take a second for germs to get in there!"

From time to time the forest opened up so that the relentless sun glared down on them. There was no escaping the heat. Ben felt his damp clothes rub uncomfortably against him; his body prickled with sweat. Even in the shade, the heat was blasting.

They trudged on for what felt like hours. He hadn't expected it to be so hard, so slow-going. The smoke had looked so close from the tree, but getting there . . . it was almost impossible.

The clicking of insects drilled into Ben's head. And he was getting flashbacks now too. He couldn't stop them. The accident. Dad.

His bad arm throbbed. His lips were dry. His tongue felt swollen in his mouth, which was full of disgusting gelatinous saliva. He needed water badly. This was supposed to be the *rainforest*! Where was all the rain? They should have done what he'd said and filled the bottle from the river. He hacked at a vine to make a passageway. No rain, only forest.

Forest.

Forest.

Now, though, the trees looked as if they had scales instead of bark. Shaggy moss ran along branches like black fur. Broken-off stumps crouched like gravestones, cupped clusters of fungus running up their edges; pale ears listening.

It definitely hadn't looked this far to the smoke from the treetop – it had seemed just a few hundred metres. Maybe they *should* have stayed by the river, tried to fix the canoe. Ben took in a big breath, imagining he could smell the burning wood of a campfire.

But there was nothing except the dank odour of rotting vegetation.

"How much further?" Rafael called anxiously. Their pace had slowed right down as Ben tried to break through the tangle of plants.

*Did I imagine the smoke?* He tapped the compass. *Are we going the wrong way?* Doubt nagged at him, grinding down his confidence. "Come on, Rafael!" he encouraged, trying to sound a lot more positive then he felt. "It's going to be OK."

Ben felt a painful ache along his machete arm, but the jaguar wound was too sore to allow him to use that arm. He didn't know how much longer he could go on cutting a trail.

Underfoot was a crust of decaying leaves that made him think of layers of dead skin. Fallen branches lay about like strewn bones. Leathery roots ran over the surface of the ground, and stems snaked round their ankles, tripping them up.

"Why did our boat have to go off the route?" Rafael complained as he hobbled after Ben. "None of this would have happened if we'd kept to my pa's map!"

Ben turned on him. It was just too hot, too hard, to take any rubbish. "That stupid map was a fake! And sorry, but we can't all be descended from conquistador Orellana!"

Rafael's voice was indignant. "That bit's true! You're just jealous! And so what if the map wasn't real?"

Ben stopped, mid-chop. "You *knew*?"

Rafael flushed bright red. "I always suspected," he replied meekly. "They didn't have that kind of paper in 1553."

"You knew all along, and didn't say anything!" Ben shook his head. "Unbelievable."

"I tried to tell Pa, but he's a bit *obsessed* with finding El Dorado – he's just too busy to come here himself. He's a very important man you know!" He sat down on a log in a miserable heap.

Ben let out a long slow breath. He went over and crouched by Rafael, digging the end of the machete in the dirt. "Your dad will be worried sick about you, you know, Raffie," he said quietly.

Rafael kept his head down and shrugged.

"'Course he will," Ben went on, trying to sound sincere. "Once he knows you're missing, and thinks you could be dead." He bit his tongue as soon as he'd said the words – but oddly Rafael looked quite cheered by that idea.

"And *your* dad," Rafael said, "I'm sure he's OK." Ben gave a quick nod and looked away. "And your mum will be very, very anxious about you both."

"Mum died." Ben dug the machete tip deeper in to the soil. "Cancer. Three years ago."

"Oh," said Rafael. There was a pause. "Oh." There was another, longer pause and then he piped up again. "What did she look like, your mum?"

Ben stopped for a moment, leaning on the handle of the machete, and wiped the sweat off his forehead. He saw her smiling face in his mind. "She had short, dark hair. Similar colour eyes to mine. The green bit, anyway."

Raffie stared into Ben's face. "Green, yes." He leaned a bit closer, frowning. "They are a bit weird, your eyes. Haven't never seen ones like that. Got sort of funny orange bits in them, too."

"*Amber*, thank you, Rafael," smiled Ben. "Green, amber. . . Only colour missing is red – with that I'd be like a set of traffic lights!"

Raffie frowned some more as the joke sank in, then nodded, chuckling.

Their laughter died away. It seemed out of place in the vastness of this forest.

They pulled themselves up and continued on in silence, trudging between the soaring tree trunks and through thick undergrowth, Ben slicing the net of branches. The forest was more compacted here, even slower going. The canopy thickened over them, blocking the light. In places it was so dark they could hardly see the way ahead.

"Careful!" Rafael babbled. "If there's a dangerous creature, we won't see them attack!"

Through gaps overhead, Ben could see that the light was fading fast. Night came quickly this close to the equator, he'd learned from their days of travelling. A dimmer switch and a click and they'd be plunged into darkness.

He struggled on, weighing up their options. His head throbbed. Should they stop and make a shelter before it got too dark, and sit out the night? But the people where the smoke was . . . what if they moved on before he and Rafael could reach them?

He had to get help for Dad. No; there was no choice but to continue, fight their way through the forest. Ben's wounded arm tensed by his side like a dead weight.

"I read that there are these snakes that can eat a man whole, and. . ."

Ben blocked out Rafael's rantings and tried to focus on just that small piece of jungle in front of him, forging a way through, one plodding step at a time.

". . .and there are these ants that use your flesh as a fertilizer to grow fungi, and. . ."

Ben checked the compass. *How much further?* His headache had got worse; his body felt heavy and clumsy.

He felt his eyelids droop. His arm was hurting more by the minute, one wave of pain followed by another. And he was strangely cold, despite the muggy air. His throat felt dry and raw. His tongue was bloated, as if he wanted to be sick. The forest had taken on a shimmery appearance. Branches seemed to shift out of the way at the last minute, then weave themselves into an even tighter screen.

"Ben, you look bad," said Raffie. "Pale, like a ghost."

He thought he heard the sound of a river somewhere ahead of them. Was he imagining it? He licked his parched lips at the idea of all that water. Then there were other sounds. Sounds that made the hairs at the top of his spine stand up. Voices?

Whispers, *like spirits*.

But Rafael must have heard them too. "What if they're not friendly?" He sounded frightened. "I read a book about cannibals, and they used to cook people's. . ."

All at once they broke out into a clearing, tumbling forward into the space. Ben saw a campfire. A group of men. Some painted with black and red. All looking straight at them.

One with a gun pointed right in Ben's direction.

# 6
# PROFESSOR ERSKINE

Ben saw a tall, elderly man come forward from the shade, a look of surprise on his face.

The man was dressed in an uncreased white cotton suit and wore binoculars round his neck like royal regalia. In one hand he held a tin mug of what looked like tea. A smoking pipe hung from his mouth as he frowned at them.

Ben stood there, staring at the vision: the trimmed beard; the grey hair combed neatly into place. Was this for real? His wound felt hot and his head throbbed. The din of insects in the surrounding forest sounded amplified. There seemed to be a shifting haziness over the scene.

He saw Rafael leaning against a hammock strung between two green canvas tents. He was looking at the man and gaping like a fish, as if he had suddenly come face to face with God himself.

"I'm Professor Erskine," the man said.

Ben felt his legs buckle, and the professor helped him to a nearby chair. "Water for the boys!" he shouted to the people round him. He gestured at individuals, making quick introductions. "My research team. Locals who assist me. And Luis from the States." A lean man with a dark blond ponytail twisted the top off a plastic bottle of water and handed it to Ben.

Ben gulped the water down – too fast, almost choking, enjoying the coolness against the back of throat as he tried to clear his head. "My dad," he stuttered. "We have to find him!"

"Why don't you tell me what happened?" said Professor Erskine gently.

Ben nursed his arm, covering up the place where the blood had seeped through the fabric, as Rafael blurted out their story between mouthfuls of water. ". . .and I forgot to tell you, Ben rescued a j—"

"A steel wire across the river, you say," Erskine interrupted, studying the location on a map. "Diabolical," he muttered. "And with children aboard."

"It was done deliberately!" cried Rafael. "To stop us finding El Dorado!"

"We don't know that for sure, Raffie," said Ben. It was so cold! His teeth chattered.

"Your father felt he was close to some kind of breakthrough, Ben?" the professor asked.

Ben nodded. How could a tropical forest be so freezing? "He had aerial photos that showed a new site."

The professor leaned in a little closer towards him. "Did any of his research survive?"

Ben had a flashback to the accident: the explosion; the

sinking skeleton of the boat. "It can't have done," he said quietly.

Erskine shook his head. "Tragic. Even today, teams exploring for El Dorado disappear. Your accident was probably sabotage. Some rival team – who can say?"

"They're probably still after us!" said Rafael dramatically. "Wanting to torture us for information! Now, I was telling you about Ben and the j—"

"Please can we find my dad?" Ben got shakily to his feet. "Can we get a search party organized. Please, Professor?"

"What you need to do, Ben, is rest a while," the professor said firmly, steering him back to his seat. "Have some food." He gestured at the fire, where a spit of meat was cooking, fat sizzling into the flames. "You've got to look after yourself in this terrain." He flipped open a jagged hunting knife and sawed off a slice of pink meat – but just the thought of food made Ben feel ill.

"Now, about Ben. . ." said Rafael, chewing his meat hungrily.

Ben felt his stress levels rise off the scale. Didn't they get it? He couldn't bear the thought of them sitting round eating a roast dinner when his dad was out there somewhere, alone, maybe horribly hurt. "Please – we have to get a big search organized!" he said. "*Now*, before it gets dark! You found it on the map? It's not far, really. Your men will know trails – won't they, Professor?" Deep aches racked his muscles. "We can pay for it! Just as soon as we get back to London and. . ."

"I'll send a runner tomorrow," the professor said vaguely.

"We'll get the word spread and find your father in no time. He was a strong swimmer, yes? He could have got himself safely to shore."

"Yes, but who'll be searching?" Ben tried to think, his headache worsening. "Could we maybe get back to the place the boat sank, and look around the rapids?"

"It'll be dark by the time we get there, Ben."

"Please . . . can't we take torches or something?"

Professor Erskine shook his head with a sigh, folding the map up. "Ben. As you know, the terrain back to the accident site from the bottom of the rapids is very difficult to cross. There's a wide pocket of a particular vegetation that even machetes can't penetrate. We need to be realistic. Getting back to that part of the river will involve a roundabout hike through easier forest. Twenty kilometres or more. The men will have to wait until morning."

It was as though little explosions were going off inside Ben's skull. *What was Professor Erskine saying?* He took a few steps, and then fell to his knees with a cry. There was a flurry of movement around him. He felt himself being lifted on to a hammock, saw the flap of mosquito nets being hung overhead.

"Burning up with fever," he heard the professor say.

"Yes!" exclaimed Rafael. "That's because—"

But the professor motioned him to be quiet, coming close to where Ben was lying. "The search will soon be under way," he reassured him quietly. "You have my word."

Ben turned fitfully on to his side. Already the sky above the camp clearing was a purplish blue, the sun gone from

view. He chewed at his nails. If Dad wasn't found tonight. . .
He saw Luis toss another log on to the fire and there was a
shower of embers, and Ben was reminded suddenly of the
way the sparks had spiralled up from the burning boat. He
broke into a fit of shivering coughs.

The professor frowned. "What's that blood on your
shirt, Ben?"

"That's what I've been trying to tell you!" Rafael cried.
"Ben's hurt! A jaguar got him and his arm bled really badly.
We need to stop it getting infected! Show him, Ben!"

"A jaguar?" Erskine strode over to Ben and pulled back
the netting. "Let me see, boy," he said with authority. He
held Ben's wrist, and eased up the sleeve. He started to
unpeel the bloody bandage from the right forearm.

Ben bit his lip. Even the lightest touch on the skin sent
tsunami-sized shocks through his whole body. He heard
Rafael tut anxiously, then gasp. He stole a sideways look.
His arm was a mess of dried blood and seeping pus, the
jaguar's claw marks clearly visible as four scarlet lines.
"I let it go," Ben mumbled. "And as it came out of the
cage. . ."

The camp had gone very, very quiet. Even the crazy
clicking of insects seemed to have died down in that
moment.

Professor Erskine was the first to speak. "Let me
understand what you are telling me," he said slowly. "You
had a jaguar in a cage with you in the rapids, and then you
released it?"

"A black jaguar," stuttered Ben. "It had eyes different

colours. One was green and the other was a kind of amber, and. . ."

The air buzzed with whispers as the local men broke into conversation – quarrels. Ben heard snatches of broken English:

"*Freed the black jaguar. . . Given its mark.*"

Ben felt the tension, as clear to him as the hot breeze rippling through the camp.

"*Mark of the jaguar,*" the murmurs went on. Some men looked at him suspiciously; others shook their heads. One stepped back, upsetting an iron cauldron from the fire.

Erskine barked out a sharp rebuke and the men fell silent. He gripped the handle of the cauldron with a piece of cloth and lifted the heavy pot back upright with a deft swing of his arm.

Ben's teeth chattered. He was so cold. So sleepy.

"The fever's getting worse." The professor took hold of Ben's bad arm again and peered at the wound. "Strange that the infection took hold so fast."

"I'm fine." Ben tried to raise his head, the same word spooling through his mind, over and over. *Dad. Dad.*

"Get me water! Fresh bandages!" Erskine clapped his hands at the local men – but they just stood where they were, one talking to the professor in agitated tones.

"Why won't they do what you say?" Rafael whispered, his voice laced with worry.

"They're superstitious, these locals. They want to consult their shaman. And certainly there will be no search party until they have his advice."

"*Shaman?*" Rafael's voice was loud with alarm. Ben felt his heart race. "You mean their *witch doctor?*"

"The men merely seek reassurance. Before starting the search. His being the father of Ben."

Ben's mind was fuzzy as he tried to follow. "What's the problem?"

"Just some old story," said the professor. "Something they're rather attached to round these parts."

"What story?"

The professor dismissed the question with a wave of his hand. "The shaman is one hour's trek from here, so we need to move now to catch the last light." He shouted out instructions, and there was now a flurry of activity from the men.

"But *shamans!*" Rafael's voice rose a pitch. "I read that they make blood sacrifices, and kill monkeys to make necklaces, and chew leaves to give themselves hallucinations, and—"

"The shaman can be rather . . . unpredictable."

Ben tried to concentrate on what Professor Erskine was saying.

"But it's our only choice. Plus he will treat Ben's infection. The wound is beyond my expertise now, I fear. It can't be allowed to get worse."

"What's wrong with antibiotics?" protested Rafael. "Don't you have any medicines? Ben can't trek for another hour!"

"He'll be carried." Professor Erskine shouted more instructions to the men. "And I'll give him something meanwhile to take down the fever."

Ben's arm was on fire. "The shaman's a doctor, then?" he croaked.

"Not only an excellent healer, Ben." The professor's face came close. "He's what you might call a bridge." The man gazed past him a moment, his eyes glinting with some secret inner thought as he spoke. "A bridge between the human and spirit worlds. His authority is never questioned.

"Now!" The professor clapped his hands. "We go!'

# 7
# SHAMAN

Ben sat up and stared at the place they'd brought him. Small fires. Lamplight. Professor Erskine and his men were sitting nearby, talking in subdued voices, Rafael with them.

All Ben could remember from the trek here was the sway and creak of his stretcher. Falling in and out of a fitful sleep. Torchlight glittering against the dense canopy. There were gaps of a pale night sky; glimpses of a nearly-full moon.

The medicine the professor had given him before they left had numbed the pain temporarily. But now his arm was in agony, and he felt groggy.

As his eyes adjusted he saw they were in a clearing, torches burning round its perimeter, and in its very centre stood a tree.

Ben caught his breath.

An enormous tree, leafless, ancient, its gnarled dead branches twisting upwards. A vast hollow tree, bark charred black as if it had once been struck by a bolt of lightning.

And in the trunk, Ben saw a thin entrance, half-hidden by vines. Someone moving inside. *The shaman?*

He started to get up, but the professor put out a firm hand to stop him. "We must wait, Ben. The shaman will see you when he is ready."

"Why can't we see him now?" Ben asked. The sooner the shaman agreed to the search, the more chance Dad had.

"The men tell me he is communicating."

"With the *spirit world*," Rafael added with a nod, eyes wide.

The professor's voice was very firm. "Ben, believe me, even if you went in there now, he would be unable to speak to you."

"They said he's taking on the spirit of a bat," said Rafael excitedly. "And making a journey to the underworld to talk to the ancestors!"

"And you believe all that?" said Ben.

"You will meet him soon, Ben." Professor Erskine lit his pipe and a wreath of grey smoke swirled up into the air. "We have to be patient."

Ben forced himself to breathe evenly; to stay calm. He looked into the faces of the men round the fire. He remembered their reaction to his jaguar marks. Some of them were still giving him suspicious looks. Some wouldn't even meet his eye. What had they said – something about *trials*? "You talked about a story, professor," he said. "What was it?"

Erskine puffed on his pipe. "It's story that has been in this people's culture for generations," he said. "A prophecy, if you like."

A man spoke up, and the professor translated. "One will come to free the jaguar and take its mark."

A young man got to his feet, speaking fiercely, and again the professor passed on his words. "The jaguar is a symbol of power. He is the most powerful animal spirit of the forest. He is the guardian spirit."

"One will come to make the past right," the professor translated from a third man. "The chosen one must pass the death trials. Free the unquiet spirits."

Rafael had been lapping up every word. "What spirits?" he asked with a mixture of fear and excitement. "And what are these death trials?"

But the men went silent, eyes fixed on the fire.

Ben's skin prickled. This forest was somewhere you could believe that anything was possible. This ancient place, it took hold of you somehow. It had a life of its own. Some kind of power. . . And Ben had that same strange sensation he'd had before, of the faintest of whispers, of something close by, made of moonlight; made of shadows. Something watching, waiting. Fleeting figures from far back, long ago.

"But this prophecy," Ben said slowly. "What's it got to do with me?"

The professor stopped sipping on his pipe and pinned Ben in his stare. "Why, the prophecy is *about you*, of course."

*Me?* Ben broke into a nervous laugh, which turned into a painful fit of coughing. *What is he going on about?*

"You freed the sacred black jaguar." The professor's

face blurred a little as Ben listened to him. "The one with the gold and jade eyes. It gave you its mark, but let you live."

A strange sound came from the direction of the tree. Something between a human and an animal cry. One by one, the men stood up.

"It's time," Professor Erskine told Ben quietly. "Go in. Alone."

Ben got unsteadily to his feet.

"By the way," the professor said, "the shaman knows no English."

Ben looked at him, frowning. "So how will we understand each other?"

Erskine sipped again on his pipe. "You will," he said quietly. "You will."

Still confused, Ben made his way towards the tree. Inside, he saw shadows rise and shrink, and felt his breathing speed up. He hesitated at the entrance, looking back at the professor, who nodded at him with a tight smile of encouragement. Rafael looked terrified. Ben vaguely saw Luis smoking on the edge of the clearing; the local men clustered on the fringe, watching him.

Then he stepped through the doorway.

Ben felt as if he'd gone into another world.

There was the smell of earth, smoke. A murky darkness. Thin tendrils of moonlight seeped from fissures above, and Ben peered through the gloom, trying to make things out. Some kind of candles threw out ghostly light. Masks grimaced along the curving walls. Clay objects stood in small hollows cut into the trunk: figures; people dressed like animals; animals standing like people. A small statue of a jaguar was raised on a plinth.

There was a movement in the space above him, and a small bat flitted past.

A man loomed up in front of Ben from the shadows, making him draw back with a gasp. Deep lines ran across the man's face like scars. Red and black paint covered the skin. The man had fangs painted from his lips down over his chin, and a kind of skullcap over his head – a leathery membrane of stitched wings.

*Taking on the spirit of a bat.* Ben's throat went tight as he remembered what Rafael had said. *Making a journey to the underworld.* How was that even possible? He forced himself to speak. "I need to find my dad."

The man came close and before Ben could react, he had gripped Ben's face between his palms, staring hard into his eyes. *Amber jade eyes*, a voice whispered.

Ben winced. The man had spoken to him – he'd heard the words clearly. But his mouth hadn't moved at all.

*You are chosen*, came the voice again.

It was inside his head! The shaman was speaking to him inside his head!

"That can't be true," Ben protested falteringly, trying not to sound as freaked out as he felt. "What have I got to do with this place?"

The shaman grabbed Ben's right arm, exactly on his jaguar wounds.

Ben cried out in pain. The shaman produced some kind

of claw – and before Ben could react, he used it to rip the bloody sleeve, peeling the fabric aside to expose the mess of skin.

Ben stood there shuddering as the man spoke rapidly to himself, peering at the infected marks. "Please tell them it's OK to search for Dad," Ben mumbled.

The shaman produced a jug and poured water on the wound in rhythmic movements, all the time talking in low tones, chanting, and smoothing away the blood with the tips of his fingers.

Ben cried out again, then clamped his mouth shut, fingers squeezed into a fist. "My dad," he gasped. "Can you help us?"

The shaman came close with a small clay pot. He dipped his thumb inside, then smeared thick yellow ointment over Ben's cuts.

Ben felt himself about to pass out with the pain. He tried to pull away, but the shaman's grip was like a vice. The room moved in and out of focus.

The shaman's voice was muffled, as if Ben was trying to hear under water, and now it didn't sound like only one person talking – more like several voices, a weird, high-pitched mesh of speech. Distorted echoes. . .

*Free us.*

*Redemption.*

*The unquiet spirits are gathering!* the shaman hissed suddenly. Ben saw the white gleam of his teeth.

*Those who suffered*, came the voices.

*Those who made suffer.*

*Dead because of greed for gold.*

The shaman lifted something to the light and Ben peered at it.

It was a ring. Pale gold.

Dad's wedding ring.

"Where did you get that from?" Shaking, he pulled it from the shaman's outstretched hand. *Dad never took that ring off! Never!*

The shaman's face was close to his. *Your father wanted to throw it into the water. But you stopped him.*

Ben twisted away as if he had been stung, a sharp memory unlocked in him. *Mum's funeral. The boat. Scattering her ashes into the water.* He fell back against the bark wall. How could the shaman know that – how he'd begged Dad to keep the ring? Nobody else in the world knew about that; only he and Dad.

Another kind of pain rose inside Ben then, stronger, more raw than any cuts on his arm. The question bubbled up before he could stop it. "*Is Dad alive?*" If the Shaman knew so much about everything, why couldn't he just answer that? He pushed the ring tight on to his right thumb.

It came then, like a punch to the chest. His crushing panic; his fear. He felt the shaman's hand on his shoulder and saw the look of compassion in the old man's lined face. *To be chosen is never easy.*

"I just need to know," Ben whispered.

The shaman drew away. He lit some leaves on a flame, then cast them on to the ground. Smoke rose in unfolding coils, filling the space, making Ben's eyes water.

Ben swayed a little on his feet. The room seemed to ripple, as if it were made of liquid. A shape was forming in the haze. A figure. . . "*Dad!*" Ben whispered. He reached out longingly, and the edges disintegrated under his fingertips.

*That is merely a vision*, the shaman said in Ben's head. *A sign of what could be.*

Ben took a sharp intake of breath, watching the image fade. "I don't understand," he stuttered. *Does this mean Dad is alive?* A warmth surged through him. Dad was alive! "Where is he?" he begged, his heart thudding.

*In the realm of the spirits*, the shaman answered.

The space inside the tree suddenly went very cold. "What?" whispered Ben. "Dad is *dead?*"

*Your father passed into the spirit world*, the shaman replied. *To reclaim him, you must first find the lost city.* He took a long, pitted bone and used it to draw in the ground. *The way to the living is through the city of the dead.*

The man crouched to run his fingers over the lines. *Free the unquiet spirits, and then they may give your father leave to pass through the portal once more and return to you.*

*Find El Dorado and find your father.*

"El Dorado?"

*The journey is full of dangers*, the shaman warned. *The way to El Dorado is in the hands of the ancestors. They created trials – death trials that can be overcome only by one pure in heart.*

The pain in Ben's arm had become an intense dull ache. An incredible fatigue pressed down on him. "I could never do any trials."

The shaman looked up at Ben. *But you have already.* The streaks of red and black across his face glowed with an otherworldly light. *The Trial of the Drowned Ghosts.*

Ben opened his mouth to speak, then closed it again.

The shaman nodded at him. He pressed something firmly into the chest pocket of Ben's shirt – then started to retreat into the shadows.

*Follow the flying gold by moonlight,* he whispered. *Then by next nightfall must you complete your quest.*

Ben could hardly see the shaman now. Only the whites of his eyes shone in the flickering candlelight as his voice faded away. *Go to my village. Find Yara. She knows where to find the bat's wing. The bat's wing will be your door to the trials.*

"Wait!" Ben wanted to ask more questions, but he was blacking out, his jaguar marks burning.

He fell. Felt compacted earth under him; sounds coming to fill the dark silence.

*There are voices.*

*Echoes from somewhere far away. Far back.*

*They took our precious things,* comes a voice that is many voices.

*A face melts away. Drops of gold fall.*

*Somewhere close a boy with long, dark hair tries to stop his gold arm bracelet being wrenched from him. The band is intricately decorated with shoals of leaping fish, but now the surface of his gold is melting as well; the boy looking on in horror. A strange whisper lingers in the air. A whisper that is*

*many whispers.*
*Free us.*
*Free us.*
*Free us.*
*Another face melts away.*

*The shaman waits for them to take the boy away, then again places the necklace of jaguar claws round his throat. He scratches the fangs down his cheeks and blood drips off his chin. . .*

*My four feet pad the forest. My eyes adjust to the dark, and I look through the leaves. There is the smell of wood smoke. The sound of human voices.*

*I see a tall man all dressed in white. I see him for what he is, and I have a sharp instinct to warn the boy.*
    *But fate must take its course. It must not be tampered with, and yet. . .*

*Do not show him the spheres.*

*I breathe the words to him, then move back to where I came from.*
    *But I know I must not interfere again.*

# PART 2

# THE DEATH
# TRIALS

# 8
# UNQUIET
# SPIRITS

Ben bolted upright and clutched at his face. He saw the boy with the long, dark hair mouthing something to him as he clutched the melting arm bracelet. But then the images faded away.

"Ben?" Rafael peered at him through a mosquito net. "Are you OK?" he slipped under the net to stand by Ben's hammock. "You passed out! The professor's men carried you. We put a fresh shirt on you – see? They made a camp near the shaman's tree."

Ben slowly took in his surroundings: faint dawn light illuminating the tall green wall of the tent; the low hiss of a paraffin lamp, insects sizzling themselves against it. Outside, voices, the smell of wood smoke, the clatter of cooking pots, the rattling clamour of the forest. His wounded arm felt strangely cool, and when he looked at the jaguar marks all he saw were four neat red lines.

What the shaman had told him came flooding back. Ben lay back in the hammock and tried to steady his breathing as he told Rafael everything that had happened.

"So your dad is somehow caught between our world and the spirit world?" Rafael gazed at him in amazement. "And El Dorado really does exist?"

"The shaman knew things," said Ben. He touched Dad's ring on his thumb. "Things he couldn't have known in a thousand years, Raffie!"

"El Dorado really exists!" breathed Rafael, his eyes bright. "But what are the *death trials*?" There was a tremor in his voice. "What will you have to do?"

"No idea," said Ben. He pivoted round and sat up. "But I'm going to find out! I'm going to get to El Dorado and I'm going to bring Dad back." He flexed his bad arm. Whatever the shaman had done, it was some kind of miracle.

"Wait!" said Rafael. "Before that: you said the shaman gave you something." He shifted from one foot to the other with curiosity. "What was it?"

What *had* the shaman given him? Ben patted the bulging pocket of his shirt, then took out something like a bark pouch, sealed with drawstrings. The hammock wobbled wildly as Rafael clambered forward to see, then settled into a slight sway as they sat side by side.

Ben eased open the strings, then halted so suddenly that Rafael looked at him, an eyebrow raised. Ben thought he'd heard whispers, faint voices. He shook away the thought.

He felt around in the pouch and took out two stones, each one a smooth perfect sphere the size of a large marble. He held them up to the white glare of the paraffin lamp.

One was a milky turquoise green with a translucence to it; the other was a golden colour with darker, honey-coloured streaks.

Ben stared at them, mesmerized. They sat in his palms like two tiny planets. In that moment they were the most beautiful objects he had ever seen in his life.

"That green one's jade!" Rafael exclaimed. "I recognize the stone. The other one's amber. But why did the shaman give you those?"

"No idea." Ben slipped the stones back into the pouch, curling his fingers round them protectively. He was filled with a strange sense of purpose; apprehension. Whatever the spheres were for, they were precious, he knew that much. He took a sharp breath. He had a strange, sudden instinct not to show them to anyone else – to keep them hidden. Where had that thought come from? All he knew was that it had come suddenly into his head; sharp, like a pain; somewhere between a shout and a growl.

"Good morning, boys!"

Professor Erskine's head appeared round the flap of the tent, followed by his hands, holding two tin mugs. "Tea?"

He inspected Ben's arm. "Healed up nicely. Our shaman certainly knows what he's doing. You see the power that man has now, Ben?" Erskine drew up a chair. "I've got to admit I'm curious. What did he tell you?"

He listened without interrupting as Ben told him everything, only missing out the bit about the spheres. "I've waited my whole life. . ." Erskine said at last. There was a wild excitement about him. "I always believed in that legend. The black jaguar." He quickly regained his composure. "Imagine, Ben! You will find your father! Free him from this limbo state he's in."

A smile spread across Ben's face. *I'm going to find Dad!*

"This Yara he told you to find – she is the shaman's granddaughter," the professor explained. "We'll trek to her village, as soon as we're ready. There's a reasonable – if rather long – track between the shaman's tree and there. We'll just have to wait while my men strike camp. "Breakfast!" he shouted through the tent flap.

Soon Luis appeared, carrying two steaming bowls. Ben noticed a rifle strapped over the man's back.

"For hunting," the professor told him, as if reading Ben's thoughts. "Luis never misses, do you? Got something for our breakfast."

Luis didn't answer, but handed them each a spoon and then went out with a small smile, whistling some classical tune quietly to himself.

The smell of food brought a flood of saliva into Ben's mouth as he looked at what was in his bowl – a kind of green-leaf soup with chunks of meat floating in it. He realized how long it was since he'd eaten, and got stuck in.

While they ate, he watched the professor open a thick book with a red cover and write in it.

"Is that research?" asked Rafael, mid-spoonful. He lowered his voice. "What kind of research do you do here, Professor?"

The professor slipped the red book into an inside pocket

of his jacket. "Archeology." He knocked some old tobacco from his pipe, then pressed a fresh wad into its bowl and leaned back in his chair.

Rafael looked about him, frowning. "We should keep our voices down," he said. "We don't know who might be listening – we've already nearly been murdered once! You are looking for El Dorado too?"

The man's bronzed face broke into a small smile. "Isn't everybody looking for that elusive city?" He struck a match and lit his pipe.

"Do you know that my great-great-great-great-great-great grandfather was a Portuguese conquistador?" asked Rafael proudly. "I had lots of research about him." His face fell. "But I lost my notebook in the boat accident."

"Can't have that!" The professor felt around in a pocket of his jacket. "Here." He produced a little hardbacked green book with a pen attached on a string.

Rafael clutched it as though it were the holy grail. "My pa had a map to El Dorado," he said. "But it was a fake."

"There's plenty of counterfeit material flying around," consoled the professor. "It can be very easy to be tricked. Many believed, for example, that a so-called Manuscript 512 written by a Portuguese soldier of fortune was certain proof that a secret city existed."

"*Historical account of a large, hidden, and very ancient city without inhabitants,*" recited Rafael excitedly. "I've heard of it!"

The professor puffed on his pipe. "Many spent years in the Amazon searching for El Dorado. One famous gentleman called Percy Fawcett coined the rather secretive name 'the City of Z'."

"*Difficulties be damned!*" cried Rafael proudly; he seemed to have forgotten that there could be murderers watching their every move. "That was Fawcett's motto!"

"That's right!" The professor laughed a deep, warm laugh which even Ben joined in with. "Few believed that many people could live in the Amazon basin," he went on, "the soil being so poor in nutrients – don't be fooled by all this lush vegetation!" Smoke from his pipe circled round his head. "Now we've evidence that there were tens of thousands, indeed perhaps even hundreds of thousands! A complex and sophisticated civilization. So what happened to them all?"

The professor snatched an insect from the air and crushed it between his fingers. "The sorry fact of the matter is that their numbers were decimated by European contact." He gave a sigh. "Their precious gold artefacts stolen and systematically melted down. Their populations devastated by diseases they had no resistance to. Their homes destroyed and whole families murdered. Those were brutal times."

Ben felt his jaguar marks throb. He had that uncomfortable feeling again, of something close by: something alive, though not living. He remembered the vision he'd seen when he was with the shaman – the melting gold face. The boy trying to stop his precious arm bracelet from being stolen and destroyed.

The canvas of the tent gave a wobble and sagged a little as the men outside began to untie the guy ropes.

"Looks like it's time to go." The professor got smartly to his feet. "Care to join me, my soldiers of fortune?"

Ben came out into the clearing after the long trek, and saw the professor's men put down their loads. They had reached their destination, Yara's village. He rolled up his sleeves to cool down as he looked round at the cluster of wood-and-thatch huts on the riverbank; the fallen tree jutting out of the water. *Hang on*, he thought. He recognized this place.

"Espírito," confirmed Rafael, panting. "The village we passed on the boat!"

Ben nodded. It kind of made sense. They must have done some sort of loop back. He swallowed hard. It all seemed so long ago, when their boat got stuck on that sandbar – like centuries ago, not just yesterday.

People came forward to greet them: women with bead necklaces, in loose cotton dresses. Men in short woven skirts. Many had their faces painted in red and black swirling patterns. The professor's men were welcomed home by their families.

Several of them greeted Professor Erskine as if he was a long-lost friend. He shook hands, smiling, exchanging words in the local language. Children were nudged forward so he could pat them on the head.

Only one person kept his distance, Ben noticed: an older man, with a headdress of yellow and black feathers. He stood by himself, by a large hut in the centre of the clearing, eyeing them suspiciously – staring particularly hard at Ben. It gave him the creeps.

"That's the chief," the professor said, heading for the man. "I need to speak to him."

"I remember you." A girl appeared, hair tumbling to her shoulders, a band of red painted across her forehead and swirling black lines on one cheek. It was the same girl Ben had spoken to from the boat. "I heard about the accident," she said earnestly, her face clouding with concern. "And that your father is missing."

Ben nodded.

"Word spreads fast," the girl added. "The sky was strange afterwards – from the smoke, I think. Some of my people went downriver to look, and they found wreckage. And the captain's body."

So it *had* been his dad he'd seen jump from the boat! Ben suddenly felt guilty for feeling so glad. The captain had been nasty . . . but had he deserved to die? It seemed Dad had escaped into the water. And so what had happened next? Had he somehow been taken to El Dorado?

For a moment the girl looked right into his eyes, and Ben felt himself blush. Then she gazed at the marks on his arm. "Many are suspicious of you." She looked at him, all serious. "They do not believe, or they are afraid. They are calling you Jaguar Boy." She erupted into giggles.

Ben grinned back. "How come you speak such good English?"

"Oil prospectors are always coming to our village," she told him. "Most of them Americans. I learn quickly!" She half-turned. "So, how is he?" She gesticulated emphatically. "My grandfather! I have not seen him for *so many* days! They tell me you went to see him."

Ben stared at her. "The shaman is your *granddad*? You're *Yara*?"

"You'll know all about the legend, then, Yara," Rafael interrupted, rushing to get his notebook open and his pen poised. "First: what are these unquiet spirits all about? If Ben's going to free them, he needs to have a bit more info about what he's dealing with."

"Don't you know?" asked Yara.

"*Those who suffered.*" Ben repeated the shaman's words carefully. "*Those who made suffer. Dead because of greed for gold.*"

"They are the spirits of our people, and the spirits of the people who came to do them harm," explained Yara. "They are forest people – our ancestors and those from other tribes. Soldiers, too. Very bad things happened in the past in the Amazon; to explorers as well. Thousands died over the years – tens of thousands. Now all their spirits haunt the jungle, yearning to be at peace."

"Conquistadors as well, I expect?" asked Rafael meekly.

Ben felt goosebumps on his skin. This was heavy. "But why is all this jaguar stuff happening now?" he asked. "After all these centuries?"

Yara shrugged. "I do not know. So much forest has been destroyed in these years; perhaps the jungle is no longer a sanctuary. But my grandfather told me he feels the spirits gathering close by, coming together from far places."

"But what are they gathering *for*?" asked Rafael,

scribbling notes.

"That's why Grandfather went to the sacred tree," said Yara. "To try to understand."

"OK, that's the unquiet spirits dealt with," said Rafael, turning to a new page of his notebook. "Secondly: what about the trials Ben has to do, Yara?" He wiped sweat from his forehead. "What exactly are the *death trials*?"

"You wanted to know about *unquiet spirits*!"

There was a hissing voice from beside Ben and he felt someone jabbing his arm. The chief was standing there, scowling in his white feather headdress. He said something angrily to Yara in the local language and she looked down at her feet, her face flushing. She lifted her head and answered back – only to get another, even sharper-sounding rebuke.

Others were listening in now as well, and the mood was spreading. There was tutting, shaking of heads; people were staring at Ben so that he felt like a freak, and he hastily pulled down his sleeve to cover the jaguar marks.

Erskine strode past the children giving them an apologetic look. He shouted something at Luis, who slowly began tightening the straps on the rucksacks as if getting ready to leave; then the two men stood together in quiet, intense conversation.

The chief faced Ben, speaking to him in deep, stern tones which Yara translated rapidly.

"I do not agree with the shaman or Professor Erskine. This boy is not even one of us! He does not speak our language – how can he be the One? The search for El Dorado has only ever brought misery and pain! The unquiet spirits must not be tampered with! Come with me and you will see." The Chief pulled at them as Yara told Ben and Rafael what he was saying. "Put an end to this idea! It will all come to no good."

Yara seemed to be trying to convince the chief. Her arms moved in an imploring way – but the elder's arms were folded firmly across his chest. He jostled the children forward.

"The chief doesn't believe what your grandfather said?" Ben couldn't understand it. "But what about the prophecy? I don't even want to be the One!" he protested. "Just find my dad. But if we don't find El Dorado. . ."

"Our chief believes my grandfather, but I think he is afraid," whispered Yara as they were herded on to a track at the edge of the clearing. "Scared for my people."

"Forward!" the chief shouted harshly from behind. Yara translated the barrage of words shooting from the man's mouth. "Nobody in our village has ever seen El Dorado. Nobody knows if it even exists! There are centuries of harm trapped inside the unquiet spirits. The caves will convince you!"

"Why caves?" asked Rafael, breathing hard. He wiped his glasses vigorously with his sleeve. "I don't do caves."

"It is where our ancestors are," Yara told him cryptically as they followed the twisting track, the chief at their heels.

Ben felt Rafael edge closer to him as they were forced on.

"The chief elder forbids me to help you," Yara said from Ben's shoulder.

Ben stopped and stared at her – provoking a torrent of

stern words from the chief.

Yara was frowning, but there was a defiant shine in her eyes. "Luciky I do only what my *grandfather* tells me," she said quietly, giving a small smile as they were marched on.

Ben touched his arm where the jaguar had cut him. It was good, feeling Yara at his side.

The trail ended abruptly and before them was the entrance to a cave: pale silver rock overhung with ferns and trailing vines. "Go deep into the cave!" ordered the chief. "See the death the search for El Dorado has brought!"

Slowly Ben walked forward, Yara and Rafael close by. They were in a passageway, and further along they could see a clay lamp burning on a rock ledge. Shadows wobbled over the stone walls as the passageway widened into a broad, high chamber, lit by more lamps.

"Is this really necessary?" Ben heard Erskine's voice carry to them from outside. "The shaman must be obeyed." Then the chief's angry voice, and a heated discussion began.

Slowly Ben moved about the chamber, letting his eyes adjust to the lamplit gloom. Then . . . his breathing started to speed up as he realized what he was seeing. He felt Rafael's hands grip his arm.

Skulls. Rows and rows of them. Each in its own alcove hewn out of the rock wall. He stared at the skulls in trepidation, their ivory-like smoothness, the empty eye sockets. The piles of bones laid alongside.

The further into the chamber he went, the darker and more pitted the remains became.

"What is this place?" Ben's voice echoed strangely as he

spoke, as if someone else were there too.

"Our ancestors have been buried here for hundreds of years," whispered Yara. "Right back to the conquistador invasions, and the ruthless search for gold."

Ben drew to a halt. As he gazed at the lines of skulls stretching back in time, he suddenly felt a powerful connection with his own ancestors, all those who'd gone before to make him who he was.

The moment passed, but the experience had shaken him. *Might the chief be right?* he thought. Was he really messing with forces that could harm others?

Some alcoves were strung across with feathers, some with fangs. Some had what looked like monkey skulls in them, all grimacing teeth, shockingly human-like.

Ben saw Rafael eyeballing a particularly grotesque face. "The chief really wants to make sure we get the message!" Rafael gulped.

"What are these for?" Ben pointed out the clay figures placed among the bones. They were like the ones he'd seen in the shaman's tree, a mixture of human and animal.

"Animals are very important in my culture," Yara said. "We believe that you can become an animal, take on its skills and attributes."

Ben was reminded of what the professor had said about the shaman. What was it again? *A bridge between the human and spirit worlds.* "That's why your grandfather was dressed like a bat," he said. "To become like the animal and be able to communicate with the underworld and. . ." He stopped, his heart beating fast. He still hadn't asked Yara! *How could*

*I have forgotten?*

"Yara," Ben began excitedly, "your grandfather said you'd know where to find the bat's wing."

She turned sharply to him. "Is that what my grandfather said? Did he really tell you that?"

Ben nodded. "He said it would be the *door to the trials*."

Immediately Yara's eyes lit up. She glanced back towards the cave entrance where the professor could still be heard arguing with the chief. She snatched a burning lamp from its hollow in the wall, then tugged on Ben's hand. "Come. Before we are seen!"

"But where are we going?"

"I know these caves," she said breathlessly, pulling him forward. "Hurry, Rafael! I have been in here many times to collect ingredients for my grandfather's medicines." She led him and Rafael through one rock chamber and into another.

"But the chief elder!" cried Rafael. "You'll get into very big trouble!"

But Yara just urged them forward more quickly, deeper and deeper into the dark labyrinth of tunnels.

# 9
# DEAD END

On Yara led them, deeper into the twisting maze of caves. Ben felt the humid, hot air of the forest turn a clammy cold as they hurried along the downward-sloping passageways. The lamp lit one sharp turn after another, and at each bend the path branched. Ben was already lost – but Yara seemed certain of where she was going, never hesitating as she chose which direction to take.

The air got even colder and Ben noticed the flame of the lamp shrink as it started to burn itself out. He didn't fancy their being plunged into total darkness in this place. And how were they going to get back with no light? He just had to trust that Yara knew what she was doing.

"The trials, Yara," Ben called as they continued on. He couldn't bring himself to say the word "*death*". "I think it's time I knew what I've let myself in for."

"Yes," exclaimed Rafael nervously. "What comes after the Trial of the Drowned Ghosts?"

"The others we do have names for," Yara replied. She

took a right into another tunnel of rock. "But they are difficult to translate. Next is. . ." – she hesitated – "the Trial of the Hanging Shroud."

"And then?" asked Rafael.

"The Sapphire Streak . . . the Howling Heights . . . and the Trial of the Guardians of the Dead."

"Guardians of the Dead?" Rafael repeated, and Ben saw him stumble a little on the rocky ground. "And what will Ben have to do?"

"Nobody knows." Yara raised the lamp to check a junction in the path, then moved hastily on. "Our legend does not tell us what the trials are, only that one must be completed to find the way to the next."

"And to find El Dorado," whispered Rafael.

"Yes." Yara paused to feel the rock surface before taking a right fork. "And once in the City there will be one final trial – but that will be revealed only face to face with the golden king himself."

"*The golden king?*" Rafael took a tumble and Ben had to shoot out an arm to steady him.

"Yes," said Yara. "But that's all I know. The story doesn't tell any more."

"Wish I had a bit more to go on," said Ben, his voice sounding faint in the echoey chamber.

The tunnel tapered, channelling them into a line – Yara first, then Rafael, with Ben at the back. They arrived at a wall of rock and a narrow gap, and Yara stopped so suddenly that they got bunched up, one behind the other.

"What now?" panted Rafael, his trembly voice amplified

in the small space.

"I have only been once this deep into the caves," Yara whispered. "And only then with my grandfather. It is forbidden for my people to venture further without the shaman." She slipped through the narrow chasm.

Ben waited while Rafael squeezed through, then followed. They just had to hope the chief never found out about this.

The roof got lower, forcing them to duck their heads to move forward. Then they were crouching, Yara's lamp making shadows flicker all around them; then shuffling through on their knees. Ben saw Yara go down on to her stomach with the dying flame held out in front, and she disappeared through a tight opening in the rock. Rafael mumbled away in Portuguese as he went next. Ben wriggled along the smooth, cold surface, following the soles of Rafael's boots. His hands shook; he felt the heavy press of rock as it enclosed him.

"Here!" Ben saw Yara standing smiling in the pool of faint lamplight as he scrambled to his feet, but beyond her it was too dark to make out anything out. He heard Rafael cough and saw the glint of his glasses. Yara darted away, and the space was bathed in a soft glow as she used her flame to light other lamps placed in alcoves along the walls.

The place Ben had stepped into revealed itself, opening up in front of him like the vault of a church. He looked around and let out a laughing gasp, nudging Rafael in the ribs with his elbow until he smiled too.

*Awesome!* Ben tilted back his head. The soaring roof was

covered in stalactite spikes. Water dripped from their tips to form round-topped stalagmites, and in places the rock had joined up to form bony columns, spangled with beads of light from glow-worms. At the far end a high waterfall poured smoothly through the chamber, the cascade disappearing into a sinkhole with hardly a sound.

Yara's lamp died with a stream of smoke, and she placed it on the floor. She pointed up the sheer rock face of the falls, and Ben saw an alcove holding a dark green plant, with strangely shaped leaves hanging from it.

"Bat's wing fern," Yara said excitedly. "It is the only place Grandfather and I have ever found it. But we could never reach it. The cave-wall cliff is much too dangerous to climb."

Ben looked at the rock face, and his heart pounded as a thought formed in his mind. He stared at the falls' white lattice of water. It reminded him of the net curtain they had in the front room back at home.

"The Trial of the Hanging Shroud," he said. Little needles pricked at his stomach.

"The waterfall – that's what's meant by the shroud, isn't it?"

"Yes!" cried Rafael. "It must be!" Then he gripped Ben's arm as he saw his friend step towards the cliff. "No! You can't climb up there! It's certain suicide!"

"I have to," Ben said simply. The words of the shaman whispered through his head and he felt their power: *Find El Dorado and find your father.*

He went to the side of the falls and tested the rock

with his fingertips. The surface was slimy, and there were patches where water oozed from the rock and trickled down. "I need to get to the bat's wing fern. The shaman said it was the door to the trials."

Yara nodded with a frown. "If that's what my grandfather told you."

"But without ropes or anything?" said Rafael, pacing about. "What if you fall? You're bound to fall! You'll be totally dead, Ben, for sure – it's a twenty-metre drop, at least! Your skull will get bashed on the rocks and your brains will splatter everywhere."

Yara had levered herself up the first section and reached out for the next handhold, but Ben called her down. "Thanks, Yara, but I'm the one who has to climb," he said. "You know that."

With a sigh Yara slithered to the ground. "But how can we help you?" she asked, biting her lip.

"Stand back and look at the rock," said Ben. His stomach churned as he thought about what he was about to do. "Tell me if you see any good handholds above me. Or anything dodgy." Mouth dry, he peered at the slick grey stone, illuminated by lamps. There were clefts up the cliff surface where he should be able to get a grip, that was true, but the flickering flames made it look as if the rock was moving, and also the surface was covered in patches of deep shadow where it was impossible to see what was going on.

"The torch, Ben!" cried Rafael suddenly. "You have one from the canoe, remember?"

"'Course!" Ben felt around in his trouser pocket, and

pulled out the head torch Rafael had given him. "Nice one, Raffie! Here, you take it. Right, shine it where it's needed. No, not right in my eyes! OK. That's it."

Rafael's chest stuck out proudly as he trained the beam. Then his voice was all worried again: "Please don't die, Ben!"

Ben took a long breath. He tried to psych himself up for what he had to do. He knew the danger; Rafael had put it pretty vividly, and if he thought about all that brain-pulping stuff too much he knew he'd never leave the ground. If this was his next trial, then he had to face it; just get stuck in.

Ben wedged the fingers of one hand experimentally into a small cleft. He found a small bump of rock near the base of the cliff and took a first step up.

Five or six metres into the climb Ben was panting, but he felt he was getting into his stride. He pushed his boots into toeholds, and continually adjusted his position to gain better balance. Spray from the waterfall gathered on his skin and his clothes, thousands of tiny spheres, slowly soaking into the fabric. Yara shouted up helpful instructions and the light from the head torch enabled him to pick out where to put his hands. His legs bent and straightened in a kind of rhythm, pushing him higher.

But soon things got more difficult. Even with the extra light, it was increasingly hard to find places to get a hold, and these were spaced further apart. The surface was more slippery as well, with slimy water running down.

Ben's tongue was clamped between his lips as he

concentrated on finding the next grip point. Sweat stung his eyes, but he didn't have a free hand to wipe it away. He felt the extra weight of his sodden clothes, dragging on each move. His leg muscles cramped as they took the strain; his arms felt stiff and heavy.

*Don't think too much*, he told himself, fingers trembling. *Don't look down. Just focus on the next move.*

But he felt his chest tighten. His breath came out in gasps. He was scarily high up now, but he still seemed such a long way from the fern. He'd totally misjudged the distance. Ben stopped, pressing himself against the cliff, struggling to get his panic under control. But when he tried to get going again his body didn't respond; it just stayed there, clamped to the rock, pinned in the torch's beam like an escaped prisoner caught in a searchlight.

The seconds ticked by, turning into minutes.

"Ben?" Yara called up.

"I'm fine," he shouted back through gritted teeth.

And as his body trembled, Ben felt a weird sensation. The jaguar marks. Little pulses of pain ran like electric shocks up his arm.

His fingers started to loosen and he was able to shift his legs a little. It was as if some invisible dial had turned all his senses up higher. He seemed to hear more tones in the sound of the water as it slicked past. When he looked up, he saw the bumps and grooves of the rock surface with clarity, his mind quickly drawing a mental map of the route he should take.

He could move again. His hands felt extra-sensitive

to every little nodule of rock, the texture of every small indentation. He made small gripping movements with his fingertips, and they felt more like claws than fingers. His shadow stretched up ahead of him, his shape distorted by the torch beam as if he had wings.

A strange small laugh bubbled from Ben's lips as he made a series of jerky movements upwards. Euphoria swept over him. He felt the pump of adrenaline. He was going to make it! He was going to find something in that alcove that would take him to the next trial. He was going to get to El Dorado; he was going to find his dad!

Lights from glow-worms on the surrounding walls flared brighter. Above him he saw the shelf of rock that marked the alcove where the fern was growing . . . alluringly close.

And that's when it happened.

He heard Yara give a yell. One second he was reaching up for the next handhold, the next he was clutching at air, his left leg kicking into nothing. Screams rang out. *Yara? Rafael?* His body swung sideways like a door slamming open, and there was a blur of images: the shroud of waterfall, the hollow space of the cavern, the dizzying drop.

With a cry of effort Ben wrenched himself back one-armed towards the rock and clung there, his hands inside a slender crevice, his heart hammering so hard it felt as if the force of it would push him off again. He stayed there gasping, face pressed against the wet rock. There were no weird supernatural sensations now, only the dark fall below him and the cold soaking through his clothes.

Ben had no idea how long he stayed cemented to the

rock. *You idiot*, he told himself. *Don't fool around. These trials are for real, and they're not called the death trials for nothing.*

Ben took a small step up, fighting to get back his nerve, wedging the toe of his boot into a narrow cleft. He inched higher, fingers clambering to find a hold, each careful movement sending shooting pains along the muscles of his legs and arms.

He felt something brush the top of his head – the thick leaf tips of the bat's wing fern, leathery, like damp pieces of skin. The rock sparkled in the torchlight as he reached up to grip the ledge. He pulled himself up with a shout – and found himself surrounded by green leaves with dusty pores like staring yellow eyes.

He heard Yara yelp from below.

"Well done, Ben!" Rafael shouted up. "What can you see? Tell us!"

Ben clambered on to the ledge and took a few seconds to compose himself. "Shine the torch on the leaves, Raffie!" Head buzzing, he parted the damp foliage and searched around inside.

"What have you found?" called Rafael. The torch beam bounced around crazily.

"Keep the light still!" Ben scanned inside the fern, lifting each leaf, feeling right down to root level. Then he felt around the back of the plant, a fingertip search of every square centimetre. He bit his lip and searched a second time. There had to be *something* – something that would lead him to the next trial.

Ben chewed the inside of his cheek. What if this wasn't

the right place? Might the shaman be wrong?

"Look again!" urged Yara.

On the surrounding cliffs, the glow-worm lights dimmed and disappeared. He heard the flames below splutter. Some went out. The shadows deepened round him.

No matter how many times Ben searched the alcove, and the leathery folds of the fern, he just kept drawing one big blank.

*Dad.*

Ben shivered as a cold wind sighed through the cave. He looked down over the ledge and shook his head at Yara and Rafael, seeing even from that height the disappointment on their faces. Ben stared back down the cliff to the cave floor and gripped the ledge more tightly. Climbing up would be nothing compared with the descent.

"You wait there!" Yara cried. She must have been thinking the same thing. "I will go and get help. Bring ropes."

The chief was going to have a field day over this one, thought Ben. *The trial's over, isn't it?* Before he'd hardly even started. He flexed his numb fingers and gave a small nod to Yara.

"Shine the torch!" Yara told Rafael. "Help me relight the lamps."

The beam swung away from Ben's alcove, leaving him in an inky darkness, making the rock seem to press towards him on all sides, trapping him.

And that's when something caught his eye.

He craned to see.

There was a line of light, coming through the waterfall.

Like a faint vein of gold in a sheet of white. Somehow light was getting through from the other side. Ben stared, disorientated. *How can there be light through there?* All the way through the maze of caves, they'd been descending steadily – so where could it be coming from?

And that wasn't all. The fissure of light stretched the entire way down to the bottom of the waterfall. If he hadn't been in the alcove, at the precise angle he was at, Ben realized, there was no chance he would have ever seen it.

There was something else as well. As Ben's eyes adjusted, the eerie glow from behind the waterfall picked out a ledge, precariously narrow, running from one edge of the alcove straight towards the slit of light.

He scrambled to his feet with a renewed burst of hope. *It isn't over.* "There's a gap in the rock!" he cried. "Behind the water! The crack goes all the way down to where you are! See, *there*." The torch beam zigzagged about before settling on the place he was pointing at. "You can get through without climbing. You see it?"

He saw Yara peer into the base of the falls, then turn to him, giving a wild thumbs-up.

Ben moved to the far side of the alcove and put a foot on the ledge. "See you on the other side!" And then he was sidestepping along it, easing closer to the pearly surface.

Soon he was just centimetres from the tumbling sheet of water. He had a sudden flashback to the rapids, to himself caught under the water, drowning, and he had to stop and hold on to a lump of rock to steady himself.

Ben wiped at his mouth. He stretched out a hand and

pressed his fingers through the moving screen of water, feeling the shock of cold, the force pushing down on his palm. He took another tiny step, paused, then went forward – straight into the heart of the falls.

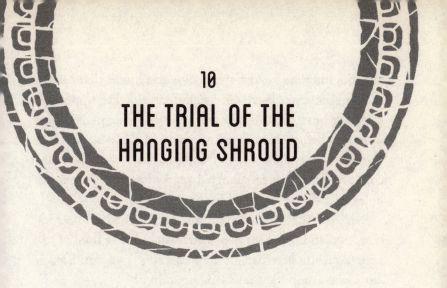

# 10

# THE TRIAL OF THE HANGING SHROUD

*"The bats were so numerous that they fluttered in swarms round the faces of our people."*

MANUSCRIPT 512

Water slammed the top of Ben's head, and he felt his knees buckle as he struggled through the falls. In an instant he was drenched, too cold to breathe. For a moment he nearly lost his balance. *Keep to the ledge*, he told himself, forcing his eyes to stay open. *Reach for the light.*

With shuffling steps he got to the fissure, gripped its edges and pulled himself in. He felt the rock grate against his chest and back as he edged through sideways. . .

Ben broke out into air and light. He let out a long shuddering gasp. Water ran down his face, and his clothes clung to him.

Coughing, he looked about him and found that he was in a bigger, even more spectacular cavern. He tipped his dripping head back to take in the scale of the place. They were well below ground, but the soaring roof was punched through with murky shafts of sunlight that looked like solid columns holding it up. Tangled vegetation trailed from the holes. His clothes steamed in the warm air.

Ben saw that the ledge he was on widened into a rock track, which made a series of switchbacks to the floor of the cave. And the best part of all was seeing Yara and Rafael, already at ground level, waving up at him!

"Awesome!" Yara shook the water from her hair as Ben reached them, spraying him with drops.

Rafael handed Ben the torch while he tried to dry his glasses on the saturated edge of his shirt. He wrinkled his nose. "What's that funny smell?"

Ben could smell it now too. A moist, earthy kind of smell he couldn't place. He shrugged and walked forward, feeling his wet boots sinking a little into the ash-like ground, coating them in a grey powder. It reminded Ben of walking on a sand dune. He felt crunchy flecks go inside his shoes and collect around his ankles, chafing the skin.

He shone the torch down and gave a shout.

The ground was alive! It was teeming with insects. Millipedes, earwigs and cockroaches, the biggest he'd ever seen, scuttled over its surface. He immediately went up on tiptoe, balancing on the caps of his boots.

Rafael was squealing, arms flailing.

"It's just guano," said Yara, holding Rafael's arm to calm

him down. She didn't look in the least bit bothered by the massive insects scuttling across her thin shoes; she just flicked them away with a deft kick. "Animal droppings." She took the torch from Ben and shone it on to a wall of the cave. "Look!"

Nothing could have prepared Ben for what he now saw. The wall was alive as well – but not with insects. Every part of it was a squirming mass of creatures; Ben couldn't see a single patch of bare rock. Leathery wings. Soft furry bodies. The wall was absolutely thick with bats.

*Bats!*

Rafael was writhing nearly as much as the bats were. "Think of the bacteria and viruses we've been stepping in!" he moaned. "And what about rabies? One bite and it's agonizing death!"

Ben couldn't take his eyes off the moving wall, the creatures jostling, clambering over one another for space. *There must be thousands of them!* It was interesting to think about, he admitted to himself – but certainly not something he wanted to think about too much. Scads of bat excrement fallen from above: food for insects who got to mega proportions.

*What now?* he thought. What was there to find here, apart from a load of poo and creepy animals? What they needed was a breakthrough.

And it was Rafael who made it.

One minute he was moving about in what looked like a cross between hip-hop and ballet dancing, the next he'd stopped stock still, feet deep in guano, his eyes alight.

"The hanging shroud!" he exclaimed. His cheeks flushed pink. "What if the waterfall isn't the shroud at all? Surely *they* are!" He waved a hand over the bat colony.

Ben eyed the dense mass of bodies. It wasn't the kind of shroud he'd have imagined in a thousand years – but the bats were certainly hanging, there was no doubt about that. Maybe Rafael was on to something. You could imagine there having been a colony in here for centuries, stretching back to when the Ancients first set the trials. "Good one, Raffie. So the question is what are those little guys shrouding?"

"I guess we need to scare them off the rock," said Yara. "It is not so nice, but necessary."

Ben nodded. "OK, then, here goes." He began to shout and clap and wave his arms, Yara joining in, then Rafael. The bats crawled about in a frenzy, their clicking squeaks intensifying.

And then at a certain point it was as if they had set off a tripwire. The bats began to lift from the wall, peeling themselves off like flakes of dark skin, turning into a massed chaos of movement.

Ben heard Rafael's piercing scream, saw Yara raise her arms to screen her face – and he barely had enough time to lower his own head and shield his eyes before they came at him.

They filled the air like smoke. He felt rough wings brush his body. Still they came, in a flapping black flood, growing outwards and upwards, spiralling through the holes in the roof of the cave.

Ben took his hands away from his face and let the bats sweep past, suddenly enjoying their closeness and the rush of air. The wound on his arm tingled, and he felt a strange exhilaration: a sense of connection with the delicate creatures.

The air calmed and Ben opened his eyes, then felt them widen. The wall was now empty of bats . . . but it was far from bare.

"Awesome!" breathed Yara.

"Raffie!" Ben whispered, grinning. "You – are – a – genius!"

There were patterns on the rock. Some kind of ancient-looking lettering.

"Hieroglyphs," said Rafael, flushing as Yara gave him a hug.

"If only we could read them," she muttered in wonder.

"Professor Erskine will be able to!" said Rafael, pulling out his notebook and copying the symbols carefully into it.

Ben ran his fingers over the hieroglyphs. He noticed that they were carved in a descending spiralling pattern, leading to a shoulder-wide, exactly square opening at the base of the rock face.

"Clever Raffie!" exclaimed Yara, crouching to look inside. "Very dark in there. It drops straight down; I can't see the bottom. But there's something!" Yara's excited voice echoed from inside. "I cannot see properly. It is not possible to reach."

"Let me see, Yara," said Ben. "Pass me the head torch, Raffie."

"It's died," said Rafael sadly, cradling the torch in his hand, then giving the casing a hefty whack. "Must have got water inside and developed a short circuit."

Ben knelt by the opening and peered inside the plunging hole. Yara was right: there was something down there, resting on some kind of ledge, but it was too dark to make out what – only the shape; it looked like some kind of box. *That was it, though! That had to be it! The clue to the next trial – it was in that box!*

Ben lay on his stomach and wriggled forward, stretching his arms, but the box was out of reach.

There was only one thing for it, Ben told himself.

He was going to have to go in head first.

"Hold my legs!" he told his friends, and he felt them grip hard as he eased himself down.

"Are you sure about this?" said Rafael. "If we can't hold you, you'll fall to your death!"

"Keep hold then, please, Raffie," said Ben. He felt his hair flop forward as he went deeper into the shaft. Now Yara and Rafael had hold of his knees. The box was tantalizingly close . . . but he still couldn't reach it. "Just a little bit more!" he shouted up.

His friends' grip shifted to his calves, then his ankles. Sweat dripped off Ben's face and down into the void. His body was hanging vertically, and he had a dizzy sensation as the blood went to his head.

Now they had hold of his boots.

Ben had a vision of his shoes slowly coming off, the way you saw in films, which always made you wonder why, oh why the silly guy hadn't thought to tie his laces more tightly before he started.

*Oh.*

"Ben!" Even Yara's voice was worried now. "We cannot hold you much longer!"

His boots were definitely slipping.

"Two more seconds!" He swiped his arm about. Now there was literally only a fingernail's width between him and the box, and if he could only shift it forward a bit, he'd get a grip. Ben strained every fibre of his body, willing himself to stretch that tiny bit further. . .

"*Ben!*" whimpered Rafael.

*Yes . . . he had it!* Did he? *Yes!* "*Pull!*" Ben shouted, and there was a wrenching and a scrambling as he was yanked harshly up.

"You got it," panted Yara, grinning.

"Yes!" said Rafael, his face bright red with the effort.

"Thanks, guys!" said Ben. "Teamwork, or what! But you nearly skinned me pulling me up!"

"*Skinned you!*" For some reason Rafael thought that was hilarious. "Skinned you!" he laughed. He rolled around clutching his stomach, hysterical, and Ben couldn't help joining in. It wasn't even funny, but it was like a pressure valve being released. Soon all three of them were in fits, their faces streaming, their giggling cries echoing round the cavern.

Ben sat back up and wiped his eyes with a sigh. He cradled the box, and the others pressed in close round him to see. It was made of smooth stone, creamy white, with no engravings of any kind; just two gold hinges, and a small gold catch on the lid – a glittering hook and an eye.

"Alabaster stone," said Rafael.

"Here goes," Ben said. "Fingers crossed we find the clue to the next trial." He slid the catch and opened the lid.

A murmur went up on either side of him. Inside was a piece of gold, about the size of his palm, exquisitely fashioned into some kind of figure.

As he picked it up, Ben felt his hand tremble. The gold had a heaviness to it he wasn't expecting. He'd once seen a design like it in the British Museum, at a South American exhibition he'd seen with his dad. The face was something like a devil, something like a man, with swirling spirals sweeping from each shoulder.

"That's a bat man!" said Yara, and Ben guessed she wasn't referring to the DC Comics version. "You know. A symbol of the connection between the human and spirit worlds?"

"The shaman was dressed as a bat when I met him," said Ben. "He told me my dad had passed into the spirit world. If I can free the unquiet spirits, then they might let him come back to our world."

Ben turned the bat over. On the back was an inlaid pattern, a simple design of three lines of gold merging into one, and he was reminded of a devil's trident.

"The clue to the next trial," said Rafael. He stared a while, then scribbled a tick list on a page of his green notebook. "*Drowned ghosts – done. Hanging shroud – done.*"

"Next it is the Trial of the Sapphire Streak," said Yara. "But what can this clue mean?"

Ben put the bat in the pouch, nestled together with the amber and jade spheres. He looked at the way the bat sent a sheen of gold light through them; then he pulled the drawstrings, sealing all three tightly inside. "Whatever it means," he said, putting the pouch away, "that's where we're heading next."

# 11

# WOVEN WATER

"It's remarkable, Ben." Professor Erskine turned the gold bat over in his hand. "The most exquisite example of a South American artefact I have ever seen. Excellent work! Now we need to work out what the clue means."

He handed it back, and Ben ran his fingers over the trident pattern engraved on the back.

"We've got to keep all this deadly secret!" whispered Rafael. "If the people who caused the boat accident find out about this. . ." He gazed round their camp. "Is it really only you and Luis who're left in the research team?"

The professor sipped from his tin mug of tea. "Yes . . . unfortunately, my local men have decided to leave."

Yara scowled. "Our chief thinks he knows better than my grandfather!"

"I would much rather have had the cooperation of your people," Professor Erskine told her sadly. "It is most unusual for a tribe to go against their shaman." He took out his pipe and pressed some tobacco into it. "But listen,

Yara. If you want to go home, I'm sure that the boys here will understand."

Ben nodded at Yara. She was already in big trouble for helping him, and he wouldn't want to make things worse. But he was relieved when he saw her shake her head.

"My grandfather wanted me to help Ben," she said firmly. "So that is what I shall do!"

"Good!" said the professor. "Now, the question is what does the engraving on the bat mean? Of course logically it should lead us to the location of the next trial."

Rafael pressed his green notebook under the professor's nose. "Might these hieroglyphs help?" he asked. "I copied them from the wall where the bats were."

The professor put the book on a folding table and bent over it. "*He who wears the mask,*" he translated, "*wears the power of El Dorado.* How fascinating." He was quiet for a few moments, as if drinking in the words.

*He who wears the mask, wears the power of El Dorado.* The words sent a strange shiver down Ben's back.

"No idea what that means," Professor Erskine said. "And not sure it helps us with where to go next." He took out his pipe and lit it. "And one would think it has to be a particular feature of the landscape that won't have changed much in the hundreds of years since the Ancients first created the clues."

"So what kind of place?" Ben asked. "Mountains?"

"Could be."

"You can get some very old trees."

"Rivers?"

"They're always changing their shape," said Rafael.

"Not necessarily," said Yara. "I mean, usually they change shape quite fast, but it depends on the type of land they flow over."

The professor nodded, puffing on his pipe.

An idea was coming to Ben; he felt his breath speed up. And there was something else he couldn't ignore. Something that seemed to link all the trials so far.

Water.

The rapids, the bat-cave falls – was that just coincidence?

"I think the engraving could be a river," he told them.

He remembered an area he'd flown over with his dad when they'd first arrived. There had been this one place – he'd taken a video of the aerial view – and he remembered his dad had asked the pilot to circle over it again, it had been so spectacular.

It was a spot where three rivers joined. And each of the three rivers had been a different colour – nothing like the usual murky green-brown .

"The rivers were gold," he told the others. "Yellow gold, orange gold, red gold! Dad said it was to do with the bedrock the water flows over."

Yara was on her feet. "I have heard of that place! It is known as the Place of the Woven Water. It is an area rich in hunting, but hard to reach. Quite far from here." She clasped her hands together. "That really could be the place, Ben!"

'I expect it will be very dangerous to get there,' said Rafael. 'But it sounds worth the journey!'

Ben could sense Erskine's excitement. "Got a map in here somewhere." He pulled over a bulging rucksack as though it weighed nothing and took out a plastic tube, from which he drew a large map. Rafael helped him unroll it across the table. The professor studied the map a while, then tapped a spot with a satisfied smile. "Here!"

"Can we set off *now*?" asked Ben eagerly.

"We leave immediately!" agreed the professor. He lowered his voice. "But let's be vigilant, my soldiers of fortune," he said.

"Yes!" agreed Rafael. "Whoever laid that metal wire across the river will be tracking our every move!"

Ben exchanged uneasy glances with Yara, as Rafael stared into the surrounding forest as if they might be ambushed at any moment.

"I have a boat moored near Espírito," the professor continued. "Did I mention that? The entire route overland will take too long. So it's boat first, then a trek. We'll have to all help with carrying supplies, now we've lost the other men. *Luis?*"

Luis nodded, whistling a classical tune as he began to disassemble the tents.

Professor Erskine gave a little laugh, and clasped Ben on the shoulder. "My dear soldiers of fortune. Great adventures lie ahead of us!"

It was Ben's first time on a boat since the crash.

He thought he'd be OK, but as the Professor's wide aluminium boat reached the stretch of water he recognized from the accident, memories of it came flooding back.

That was tough.

Luis revved the outboard motor, powering them down the safe left fork, and the boat ate up the miles along the river's wide meanders.

They took one branch, and then another, the professor keeping an eye expertly on the map, Luis steering with silent precision, Rafael keeping watch at the stern of the boat to check for signs of anyone following them.

Afternoon turned into evening; evening into night. They discussed El Dorado; Yara caught them fish; Rafael kept a careful record of their journey in his notebook. Ben beat them both at chess, then the professor beat him. Mostly they stretched out under the awning of the boat, just trying to keep cool. They passed a few trading posts; filled up on supplies and news; but Ben was always glad when they were on their way again.

*Find El Dorado and find your father.* The shaman's words never left Ben's thoughts. How would finding the lost city free the unquiet spirits? he asked himself. But the question remained unanswered.

One night passed, and then another. The trading posts petered out to nothing. The forest stood thick and full of shadows along the riverbanks.

At one point, Ben was sure he caught a glimpse of the black jaguar in the undergrowth, its green and orange eyes staring at him across the water. From that moment on he had an unnerving sense of time running out that he couldn't shake. It hung over him, heavy like the humidity and heat.

*Follow the flying gold by moonlight* – those were the words the shaman had used; then he would have only until the next nightfall to finish the trials. What had he meant by *flying gold*? Nobody had been able to shed any light on it. It was unsettling, not knowing. An unseen clock was ticking, but he had no idea how long he had left.

And could someone be following them – someone also on the trail of El Dorado?

"Are we there yet?" puffed Rafael at regular intervals, fanning himself with a sunhat. "How much further?"

But at last, late on the morning of the third day, Ben heard Luis cut the engine, drawing the boat up on a gravel shore, and the professor jumped off and landed lightly on the bank. "We walk from here. We're only five or six hours away! Luis, you clear the way, man."

Luis pulled an enormous rucksack on to his back, picked up a machete and started to cut a trail, whistling as he went.

"There's your bag, Yara. Pack for you, Rafael. And Ben." The professor lifted a rucksack off the ground for him with one hand. Ben sagged under the weight, then fiddled with the straps to try and get it comfortable.

"Professor Erskine is old," whispered Rafael to Ben. "But he's a lot stronger than you."

They started the trek, following the trail Luis cut for them. None of them spoke much. Ben concentrated on walking in the heat, getting used to his bag and getting the pace of the steps right. The forest was a sauna; the insects vicious. The professor allowed them a five-minute rest each hour, no more.

"It's like being in the army!" wheezed Rafael as they sat on logs sipping water from canteens. "Why does the professor have to be so bossy?"

Ben watched the Professor talking quietly to Luis. "He really knows what he's doing, doesn't he?"

"He knows a lot about the forest," said Yara. "He has been coming here since he was a young man. His story is a strange one."

Ben sat up a little. "What do you mean?"

"Well." Yara shifted closer and lowered her voice. "Many years ago, when he was only a small boy, people from my tribe found him wandering alone in the forest."

Rafael stopped drinking. "Really? What had happened to his parents?"

"His parents were explorers," Yara told him. "Rich people from England. Neither they nor the plane they were travelling in was ever found. Everyone assumed it had crashed somewhere, but nobody knows how he survived by himself for so many days."

Ben stared at her, letting the story sink in.

"He had a bad fever when he was found," Yara went on. "He kept repeating that he had met a man made of gold." She raised her eyebrows at Ben. "And something about being led to safety by a black jaguar, with one eye gold and one eye green."

Ben felt the hairs on the back of his neck tingle. "Do you believe that?"

"Why wouldn't I?"

Rafael gave a low whistle. "Well, that explains why Professor Erskine believes the El Dorado prophecy so strongly."

"Some say he found the entrance to El Dorado," said Yara. "Some say he is a holy man. My tribe looked after him for a while, then he was recalled to England. He returned as a young man and has been making trips here ever since – trying to find the way back."

"Luis is going ahead to make camp!" the professor called as his researcher disappeared into the forest. "Not far now!"

They continued the trek, the trail snaking upwards. Ben couldn't get the professor's story out of his mind. Losing both his parents like that. Searching his whole life for the way back to El Dorado. That kind of thing would have driven other people crazy.

Finally, after a long uphill slog, they reached an outcrop hemmed by bushes, and the view opened out. A refreshing breeze cooled Ben's hot face as he looked at the amazing expanse of forest rising up hazy blue mountains, their jagged peaks lit by late afternoon sun. He wiped a sweaty hand across his face, looking for signs of a river. Somewhere nearby he could hear water: *the Woven Water confluence?* And there was a moist smell to the air. But the twisting bank of bushes was too thick to see through, and they had some serious spines on them.

"Awesome!" exclaimed Yara. "What a panorama!" She slipped off her pack and came to join him.

Rafael lay down, rucksack still attached, and gave a smiling groan.

Across the plateau of rock, Ben saw two tents pitched, their guy ropes hammered with metal pegs into clefts. Assorted equipment was scattered around: some pots and pans, a coil of steel wire, water canteens, rope and a machete.

"Luis not here?" the professor said. "Must be hunting food for us. Make yourselves at home, my soldiers of fortune, and I'll go and find him. Sit tight and rest until I get back! The Woven Water confluence is only a short trek from here."

Ben heaved off his rucksack and flexed his aching back, and they sat, sipping water, waiting for the professor.

Rafael wriggled out of his pack straps and sat up. He gazed at the vista. "But how *can* El Dorado exist?" he asked suddenly.

Ben drummed his fingers on the rock. *How long is Erskine going to be?* "What?"

"I know we've talked about this before, but with all the modern technology we have, I mean," said Rafael. "Satellite images and mapping tools."

Ben stood up and started pacing around. How *could* any secret city in the middle of Brazil have stayed hidden all that time?

Yara's face creased into an frown. "If my grandfather says El Dorado exists, then it does! My grandfather never lies!"

"I want it to exist!" Rafael said hurriedly. "Of course I do! It's just difficult to understand why nobody's found it yet."

"Only Ben can find it!" Yara shot back. "By passing the trials!"

Ben strode over to the thorny bushes in the direction of the water. He pulled at the branches to try and find a way through, getting scratched by some vicious spines in the process. Rafael's comment had shaken him. No El Dorado meant no Dad.

The sun had dropped lower in the sky, turning the mountains the colour of fire. Purple shadows moved up their craggy slopes. It would be dark soon. A bird darted overhead, a type of kingfisher; Ben caught a glimpse of dazzling blue as it skimmed past. He looked about impatiently. "Where's the Professor?"

"Do you think something could have happened to him and Luis?" said Rafael. "If the metal-wire murderers followed us, they could pick us off one by one!"

Ben felt a twinge of worry, but dismissed it. It was just Rafael being over-dramatic, wasn't it? He got to his feet. "I'm going to find the gold rivers!" he said. "I can't just sit about here!"

"Wait for me!" said Yara.

"Don't leave me alone!" Rafael scrambled up.

Ben followed the sound of the water across the plateau to the bank of thorny bushes. "Pass me that machete, Rafael, will you?" He slashed at the plants with the blade and picked his way over the wide expanse, stopping suddenly where a dodgy-looking platform jutted over the last half-metre.

Immediately his agitated mood dissolved. Below him

was an amazing sight: three crystal-clear rivers running gently over gold-coloured bedrock into a deep basin, spilling over into one single river.

There were murmurs of amazement as Yara and Rafael drew up next to him, and Ben got out the bat and lifted the trident clue to the scene. "The colours match!" he exclaimed. "Look at that – pretty much exactly!" *This has to be the place!*

"What's that in the basin?" Yara pointed. "Can you see? In the very centre!"

Ben strained forward. It looked like a hole, yes, a circular hole. And was there something engraved on the rock around it? The pattern was hard to make out, the water magnifying but distorting.

He and Yara did a silly dance on the rock.

"Now what?" asked Rafael with a frown, sucking his finger where a thorn had scratched it.

*Yep – what now?* Ben scanned the sheer drop into the water and the surrounding landscape. That's why they'd had to leave the river and trek up here. There'd been no other way to get to this confluence.

It dawned on Ben what he had to do.

And there was only one possible place he could do it from – the thin platform of rock right in front of him.

He rubbed at his arm. The jaguar marks were throbbing, but he tried to ignore the pain. The light was fading fast. Did he want to have to wait another twelve hours until it was light again? No way!

Ben bent down and started untying the laces of his boots.

"What are you doing?" Raffie cried in alarm.

Ben unbuttoned his shirt. "I need to get down there."

Shadows moved across the forest as the sun was obscured by wisps of cloud. A movement caught his eye, in amongst the trees: a fleeting dark shape – another shadow? But then it was gone.

"You're going to *jump*? But it's so high!" protested Raffie. "We can't tell how deep the water is from here. You could break every bone in your body!"

Ben pulled off his shirt and his socks and stretched out a bare foot to test the platform – prompting another volley of protests from Rafael.

"Please think about this! That's no way stable!"

Raffie was right about that, Ben thought grimly. The surface rocked unnervingly, like an uneven paving stone, even when he pressed on it just the tiniest bit.

"You should wait for the professor!" insisted Rafael. "Him and Luis will be back any minute!"

But Ben was tired of waiting. He stepped up on to the platform and waited for the sickening wobble to subside.

Yara's face had gone very pale. "Good luck, Ben."

He dragged his eyes back to the water and moved into a dive position, feeling the whole platform move. Below him was the drop, the basin of water. If he stood there much longer he was going to lose his nerve.

The Trial of the Sapphire Streak. Why "*sapphire streak*"? he wondered.

"OK," he murmured to himself, taking a set of long, steady breaths. His toes curled over the unstable lip of rock.

"OK." He tipped his arms forward, eyes locked on to the centre of the hole. He took a last look behind him at his friends, then a long, deep breath.

And dived.

# 12

# THE TRIAL OF THE SAPPHIRE STREAK

Ben had a feeling of flying, a strange sensation of time slowed down; of being straight and streamlined, like an arrow. He felt exhilaration as the air raced over his body; the rush of adrenaline as he plunged at his target, the staring eye of the hole.

But the brief rush soon evaporated.

The cliff was higher than he'd expected, the impact much harder than he'd thought it would be. He slammed the surface of the pool and went deep. Very deep. The water hit his face like a fist. Gasping, he shot down into the colder layers of current. He felt himself decelerate and then a brief moment of being suspended. He opened his eyes, wincing at the sting of water; he saw the hole right below him and swam towards it.

Ben's arms pulled at the water, his legs kicking. He swivelled his head to look up and could see the distant rippling shapes of Yara and Rafael on the top of the gorge, waving their arms about.

*How much further?*

Ben's fingertips brushed the rim of the hole and he gripped on to it, heaving himself towards it, feeling the texture of hieroglyphs round its smooth edge. It was smaller than it had looked from the platform, maybe half a metre across. He strained to make it out through the murky water. His arm was in up to the elbow, searching; then up to the shoulder. But there was nothing he could see, nothing he could feel except the smooth, curving walls of the cavity.

A stream of air bubbles shot from Ben's mouth. There was no turning back.

Ben knew he could hold his breath; the rapids had taught him that. And he could summon up extra energy when he needed it – hadn't the hanging shroud trail shown him that? But he was wasting precious seconds.

Ben grasped the perimeter of the hole and put his head inside, then slipped both shoulders through, all the time scanning the space, hurriedly feeling round it.

*Get back up, now!* he told himself.

*Just a little longer!*

*Go back!*

He felt the rock rub his spine as he went right inside. The water was gloomy and his lungs screamed for air as he felt round the chamber.

But now something was happening above him.

Ben sensed the light change and twisted his head round to look. His eyes widened, hurting from the cold of the water. For a few seconds he couldn't make any sense of what was happening.

What *was* that?

Something was moving towards him through the water, rocking slightly as it came. It was a trick of the light, surely . . . an optical illusion because of the depth? But as he stayed there staring, suspended, Ben knew there was no doubt about it.

A thin, wide piece of rock was moving through the water. Like a lid coming down, the slab was slowly, relentlessly sinking straight towards the hole.

Ready to trap him inside.

*How? No time to think!*

Ben's cheeks bulged as he fought the need to breathe. *Find the clue! Get out!*

He frantically scrabbled at the rock at the bottom of the hole, feeling for something, anything. His muscles were heavy from lack of oxygen. It was like swimming upside down through syrup. The hole was closing. The circle of light above him was being covered over, as if in an eclipse over a sun. His palms hit out at the scoop of rock; he was using mostly touch now; mostly instinct.

Ben's chest tightened as something moved under his desperate fingers. Corners. Edges. *No more time!* Ben grasped the object.

*Head up! Get out!*

He kicked his legs, turning in the water with an agile twist; saw the light above him now dangerously narrow.

The water felt thicker as Ben struggled to reach the gap, as if it were solidifying round him. He clasped the object to his chest with one hand and clawed his way up, in one – last – effort – to – escape.

Shoulders, ribcage, spine, hips; he felt the rock scrape against him as he fought to get through. His legs slammed painfully against stone as he thrashed in the water. The rock trap gripped his feet, flexed his ankles and heaved at the water with his free hand to escape. He felt stone catch at his toes, then he was up . . . out. . .

Light spread above Ben as he made for the surface.

A blue sky, the light blue of early twilight.

Blue like pale sapphires. Blue like Dad's eyes.

But he was still too deep, the surface still agonizingly far away. It was like being trapped under a lens. Ben flailed upwards. Was this how it had felt for Dad as he'd drowned? Yearning for air but never reaching it?

*Dad!*

The water around him exploded into ripples as Ben broke the surface. He turned on to his back, arms open, and let the water hold him; mouth gaping, controlling his panic, waiting for the air to come. *It will pass.*

On the cliff he saw Yara and Rafael, and the professor and Luis. He felt his body convulse as he took in short stabbing snatches of air.

Then a laugh exploded through Ben's lips; he was gasping and laughing. It hurt to laugh, but he did it anyway. They were a step closer. A step closer to finding El Dorado! Another step closer to finding Dad! Treading water, with a coughing shout he lifted the object above his head for them to see. The last light of day glinted off the box in his hand.

Yara yelped in delight. Raffie let out a holler and waved

his arms about in a geeky dance. Ben saw the professor slap Luis on the back.

A rope spiralled down from the cliff, its end hitting the water and floating there, and Ben swam to take it.

He looped the rope around his waist and let himself be pulled up, still holding on tight to the box. One last drag and he was sliding forward on his stomach, back on to the smooth rock of the platform in a soggy heap. He rolled over and was helped up to a sitting position.

"Rather a close call, that one, Ben," the professor said, as he untied the rope.

"Thanks, guys," Ben panted.

"Your jump triggered the fall of the rock," Rafael told him, his eyes like an owl's.

"We could not believe it," said Yara. "As soon as you jumped, the platform shifted forward, and then a whole piece of it fell down after you!"

"A remarkable mechanism," the professor remarked, studying the end of the platform. "My feeling is that only someone of the right weight jumping from that exact spot would have set it off. Quite ingenious."

"Whoever designed these trials," smirked Ben, pulling on his shirt, "they really had a thing for water."

"It is getting to be something of a theme," said Professor Erskine with a smile.

"So *what's in the box*?" Yara asked excitedly

"It looks just like the first box!" Raffie said, craning over Ben's shoulder.

Ben fingered the small gold catch on the lid. The

smooth pale alabaster shone in the twilight, silvery like the scales of a fish. He remembered that moment of his dive from the platform. He remembered how it had felt as he moved through the air, that sensation of flying, and his swift, straight plunge through the water.

"Your turn to open, Raffie," Ben said.

His heart thudded as Rafael unfastened the catch. But even before his friend lifted the lid, Ben guessed what they would find.

# 13
# HUNTERS

It was another gold icon. A pure gold icon, similar in size to the bat, only this time it was a bird, with a long sharp beak and a swirling crest, and every gleaming feather exquisitely cast. Even in the fading light, Ben could see how beautifully it had been made.

"Oooh!" Raffie gasped.

"Kingfisher!" exclaimed Yara, clasping her hands together.

"An ultimate hunter," said the professor, nodding at Luis.

The five of them stared at the bird for a while, until Ben broke the silence, dying to tell them his theory. "They're connected," he said.

"What are?" said Rafael, looking puzzled.

"The trial and its icon!" Ben exclaimed. "Do you see?"

Yara looked at him. "Yes!" she said suddenly. "I understand!"

"I don't get it," Rafael frowned. "Connected? How?"

"To find the gold bat," Ben explained, "I had to act like a bat – climb the cliff, hang upside down and all that. To find this kingfisher, I had to do exactly what that kind of bird does – dive in to the water to reach a target, then swim back with it!"

"Not just *act* like a bat and a bird," the professor added thoughtfully. "*Become* a bat; *become* a bird."

"Yes," Yara agreed. "Find a bridge between the human and animal spirit worlds."

"And the next trial?" Rafael asked. "The Trial of the Howling Heights? What animal skills might you need for that?"

Ben drummed his fingers on the stone box. "Who knows? But first we need to work out where to go."

"What's the next clue, then?" Rafael could hardly contain himself.

Ben lifted the bird from the box and turned it over, and everyone leaned in to see.

On the back was a series of lines that curved into spirals at their tops.

"Trees?" murmured Ben.

The professor held the bird up, studying the design. "It does look like some kind of forest."

A full moon was rising as they got back to the tents. Luis made a fire and while he cooked they looked at maps and talked about what the clue could mean.

Ben smacked at a mosquito on his arm, leaving a smear of blood. The exhilaration he'd felt when he'd got the bird seemed to have vanished. They were frustratingly still no nearer to understanding where to go to next.

Ben stared over the forest; the outlines of branches glistened in the ghostly light. He prodded at the fire with a stick as they ate. The campfire crackled. Insects sizzled as they flew too close. The moon cast bright light and deep shadows over the camp.

The professor leaned towards the fire, so that flames were reflected in his eyes. He puffed on his pipe. "This forest clue *is* proving to be rather troublesome," he said, and for the first time Ben detected a tone of annoyance in his voice.

Everyone was looking at Ben, as if he had all the answers. He studied the map spread out on the rock, feeling the pressure of their eyes on him. He rubbed at his jaguar marks, hoping for a bolt of inspiration, but none came. He thought back through the things they'd already discussed:

*(1) The clue showed some kind of forest.*

But what kind of forest would be different enough

from the hundreds of square miles of other jungle? Ben scoured the map again, but even with the professor's numerous annotations, no areas stood out. Apart from rivers and mountains, there was only one patch on this map that *wasn't* forest. It was right at the edge of the map and labelled "*thermal area, unstable ground*", and hardly likely, as the professor had explained to Raffie, to be unchanged for centuries. Not a suitable place for the Ancients to put the next clue.

*(2) Why "howling heights"?*

Yara had suggested it was something to do with the howler monkeys that lived in parts of the forest canopy. Maybe the "howling" referred to some other natural phenomenon, thought Ben – moving water of some kind, maybe; or the sound of the wind through rocky pinnacles.

"One feels we are very close now to finding El Dorado." The professor smoked his pipe, and Ben saw his face glaze over with a look that was strangely disturbing. "That fabled city of gold."

"And finding *my dad*," Ben reminded him, looking hard at the professor.

"Finding your father," Erskine agreed, blowing smoke from his mouth. "Of course; that too." He got to his feet, rolling up the map. "I suggest we all retire to our beds," he said. "Look at the problem with fresh eyes in the morning. Mind if I keep hold of the bat and bird until tomorrow, Ben? I'd like to make some sketches of them. Take some photos as well."

"I'm not tired," said Ben, handing over the icons. It was

his turn to feel annoyed. "I want to keep thinking about the clue!"

"One needs to sleep," insisted the professor. "One may find a new day brings new answers." He gripped Ben's shoulder as he went by, and Ben felt him pinch the skin, almost hurting him. Then the man patted him on the back. "Goodnight, my soldiers of fortune. Sleep well."

But even the gentle swing of his hammock couldn't lull Ben to sleep. The sound of insects was like hundreds of knife blades scraping against each other. The heat was stifling. The din of tree frogs punctured his brain, never letting up.

*What if they couldn't solve the next clue?*

Ben bit the inside of his cheek. The jaguar wounds on his arm throbbed. He kept shifting about, thinking about his dad, trying, and failing, to find a comfortable position.

But there was something else that was bugging him; and it wasn't just worry about the clue, or the sticky heat. It was the Professor. When Erskine had been talking about El Dorado and its gold – that look on his face in the firelight. It had been a look of real greed. Ben was sure he hadn't imagined it.

Time dragged. Ben dozed. Then suddenly he opened his eyes. There were noises outside the tent – agitated whispers. "*Not here!*" a voice hissed. "*Do you want the children to find out?*" Then the sound of footfalls moving away.

Moonlight shone on the skin of his tent and Ben saw two moving silhouettes. The distinctive profiles of the professor and Luis.

*Find out what?* Wide awake, Ben swivelled his body noiselessly. He slid his feet to the ground and lifted his mosquito net to slide through.

Slowly, slowly he raised the flap of the tent and looked out.

Professor Erskine and Luis were walking away across the outcrop. Where were they going? He heard their low voices, but couldn't tell what they were saying. He slipped after them.

They had descended a little into the forest and Ben edged forward, keeping to the shadows. Insects bit at his face – and who knew what might be waiting in the darkness between the leaves? But he had to find out what they were up to. *This doesn't feel right.* He parted the waxy, dark foliage and looked through.

"It's strong enough to crush bone." An American accent. It was the only time Ben had ever heard Luis speak.

"The pelt must not be damaged." The professor's voice had a tone he hadn't heard before either: tight, angry. Ben's breathing speeded up. *Pelt?*

"I've put four of these beauties along the trail." Luis heaved up a metal object.

*Luis has a lot to say tonight*, thought Ben. He strained forward, seeing two curved pieces hinged at one end, each lined with a row of stained, jagged points.

Ben's scalp crawled. It was some kind of evil-looking trap.

"I don't want any more mistakes."

"The wire did exactly the job you paid me to do," Luis replied defensively. "We got rid of another rival."

*Wire? Rival?* Ben's shoulders tensed. It was all starting to make horrible sense.

The fire, the explosion. . . Erskine had told Luis to cause that?

Ben remembered the metal wire he'd seen at Professor Erskine's first camp. The figure he'd seen watching their boat before the accident – had that been Luis, checking the results of his work?

And what had Erskine said about El Dorado research teams disappearing? All along, he'd been trying to make out that someone was after them, the liar!

And it can't have been the first time he and Luis had tried to kill someone.

Ben curled his fists. He'd been tricked. He felt a mad urge to run out and confront Erskine there and then.

*Use your common sense*, a voice inside him warned. *They've already tried to kill you once. You're all in danger.*

"How was I to know his boy was the *One*?" Luis's voice was thick with sarcasm. "Anyway, he survived, didn't he? He'll lead you straight to the mask."

*Mask?*

A night breeze ruffled Ben's hair, and his back felt sticky under his shirt. *What did he mean, mask?*

"The boy survived thanks to fate, not to you!" the professor snapped. "There are forces way beyond you at play here – ancient powers you cannot even begin to understand. You just do what I pay you for, and keep quiet!"

Ben felt his face go hot. All Erskine wanted was to use him to find El Dorado!

"And if it wasn't for your blunder," Erskine continued, "I'd have the black jaguar pelt by now!"

Ben swallowed a gasp. He remembered the captain's words: *I already have a buyer for that skin.* The *professor* wanted to kill the black jaguar. And the disgusting animal trap Luis had now. . .

He saw Luis prod the metal with the tip of his boot. "Elusive that cat is, after it got caught the first time," he said. "Hard to track. There's something strange about it. It's high-risk. So to bring up the topic of pay. . ."

"We agreed a share of the gold once we're in the City," the professor retorted. "I've been more than generous."

Luis paused before he replied. His voice had a hard edge to it. "I've slightly changed my mind on that front, though. Seeing how this mask is so important to you. Thought I'd get a share of that as well."

The next moment, Ben saw the professor spring towards Luis with startling speed. He had him by the throat, pinning him against a tree trunk. A flurry of grey insects flew from the bark as he banged the hunter's head against it. "The mask is mine – and only mine!"

Luis said nothing. Just gave a short nod, the whites of his eyes lit by moonlight.

The professor released him and straightened the cuffs of his jacket. "And it must be the black jaguar – not *that* kind!" He gestured dismissively towards a nearby patch of trees.

Now, for the first time, Ben saw something there, hanging from a branch. He peered into the shadows, then felt a stab of nausea. It was a cub, gold-coloured, with a pattern of black diamonds through its fur. A jaguar cub, strung up by the neck; dead eyes wide.

"The pit's ready, too," Luis said. "Only something over a certain weight will set it off."

"Just make sure I get the adult male next time," the professor spat, "not some pathetic cub! I have to wear that pelt, understand?"

Luis narrowed his eyes, but said nothing.

Seeing the dead cub shocked Ben into action. He edged backwards, away from the men. He had to tell the others; make a plan!

But the animal they were hunting. . . *The jaguar Ben had saved!* Why did the professor want the skin so badly? Whatever the reason, Ben wasn't going to let that liar catch his black jaguar!

Ben bit at his fist. He was going to get rid of those traps. Every one of them! There were still plenty of hours of darkness left. Time to find the traps; then escape with Yara and Raffie. Luis had said there were four of them, right? All placed somewhere along the trail they'd come in on.

Ben got to work, using the moonlight on the trail to guide him. He found a long, thick branch and trod slowly, checking each footfall and probing with the stick. The thought of those metal teeth made him shiver a little, despite the muggy heat. The last thing he needed was his own leg caught in them.

He found the first trap by a turn in the trail, placed in a small hollow along the edge of the track, its jaws stretched wide. *Set it off.* Ben scoured round for what he needed and found a heavy chunk of wood, which he rammed down on the metal teeth with all his weight. There was a sickening splintering of wood as the log was crushed.

The trap was heavy, a lot heavier than it looked; solid iron. With a grunt of effort Ben lifted it and lobbed it into the undergrowth, hearing a satisfying *whump* and the cracking of branches.

He found another trap – then another, noticing a pattern to their spacing.

After getting rid of the third trap, Ben stood there, panting. Just one left now. He paced the distance to the next, but found nothing. Could he have missed it? He backtracked, checking the trail and its fringes.

*This is taking too long!* He had to find that last trap!

Ben started to jog, eyes trained on the moonlit path ahead, concentrating hard on where he was stepping; what he might be stepping on. He still had the head torch and put it on to illuminate the patches of shadow. His shirt stuck to him with sweat. His feet pounded the ground, as fast as he dared, searching, searching. . .

And then, as the track snaked to one side, Ben skittered to a stop. There it was, the final trap gaping on one side of the path like the dislocated jaws of some grotesque reptile.

A small smile broke over Ben's lips. He picked up a heavy branch and moved forward to attack.

But suddenly the ground softened, making his legs buckle under him. For a brief moment, Ben thought he'd stepped in a swampy pocket, but now the ground was shifting, creaking, snapping, moving downwards. Leaves flew past; broken branches grazed him as the forest floor gave way. Ben clutched about wildly, finding only loose sticks and air. The deadly trap flew past his face.

And then he was falling, falling. . .

His chest slammed the ground. Head struck hard.

Then nothing.

*There are voices.*

*Echoes from somewhere far away. Far back.*

They made us ill, *comes a voice that is many voices.* Help us!

*There is groaning, coughing; people struggling to breathe.*

"I'm coming," Ben calls. *He tries to get to them; fighting to pass through the dark, waxy leaves.*

*He see their eyes, lit by moonlight, pairs of eyes like marks on moth wings.*

*A little girl turns towards him and stretches out her hand, and he sees that her round face is a mask of raw welts.*

*"Help us," she whispers to him.*

*The eyes burn gold and green, then merge to black.*

*A strange whisper lingers in the air. A whisper that is many whispers.*

*Find the golden king.*

*Restore his power.*

*Free us.*

*Free. . .*

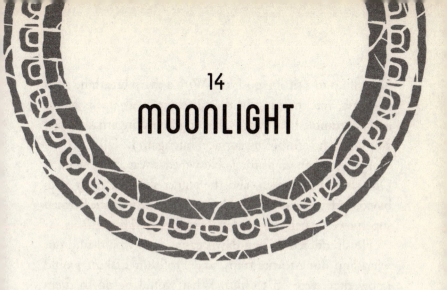

# 14
# MOONLIGHT

Ben woke. His teeth were clenched against something cold and soft. There was the gritty taste of soil in his mouth. The smell of rotting vegetation made him gag and a painful spasm racked his chest. He became aware of night sounds: the clatter of insects; wind through tree branches; the booming howl of monkeys.

Ben opened his eyes, and black slowly became grey, then silver. He lifted his head. Moonlight shone from a hole several metres above him. A coldness crept along his damp back. The animal pit Luis had dug!

Ben tried to control his breathing. How long had he been unconscious for? *Yara; Raffie. They're in danger.* He had to get to them; tell them about the professor.

Ben shifted his body experimentally. He ached all over, but there were no stabbing pains – maybe he'd been lucky and not broken anything. The ground felt slightly moist, a bit squidgy; maybe that was what had softened his fall.

He moved on to his side with a grunt, then dragged

himself up to a sitting position. With a sharp breath he tried to climb, but the mud of the pit came away in his hands and he stumbled backwards. He dug in his fingernails to get a hold on the crumbling surface, but again he fell.

Ben stood there panting. He wiped sweat from his face. One cheek felt swollen, and the tender skin was tacky with blood, with grains of dirt sticking to it. Where were the Batman superpowers when you needed them, he asked himself?

He shuddered. When dawn came, Luis would find out what he'd done to the traps, and Professor Erskine would know they were on to him. What would he do to them then – to Yara and Raffie?

Ben felt like shouting at himself for being so stupid. *We should have got away when we had the chance!*

It wasn't even as if they knew where to find the next trial! The clue on the bird had led to a dead end.

The earth came away in Ben's fist and he fell again, slamming back on to the floor of the pit. It was impossible!

The distant howling sounded again.

Ben hit the wall with his fist in frustration, bruising his knuckles. *Stupid!* Then again, biting his lip with the pain. But as he brought his hand to strike a third time, he stopped. Something had caught his eye – something on his thumb, reflecting the moonlight. He looked at it, panting.

Dad's wedding ring. He fingered the glinting gold circle.

Ben rested his forehead against the wall of earth. This was how it had felt. After his mum had died. Like being in a pit. A pit you think you will never climb out of, because you're down so deep and you feel so lost.

Tears pricked Ben's eyes, but he swatted them away. He'd got out of that hole. Somehow he'd done it. Little by little. He and dad together, doing the impossible.

Ben felt his heartbeat steady. Dad was the only family he had left, and he had to help him. Somehow he was going to free himself from this pit as well, and carry on the trials.

Then Ben saw something else glinting in the moonlight, and he recognized the trap that had fallen with him, its jaws firmly clamped together.

Hands trembling, he studied the mechanism.

He gouged a sharp-edged stone out of the ground with his fingertips and used it on a screw of the hinge. At first the head wouldn't turn at all – but suddenly it shifted, and by twisting the stone hard, he managed to get it out.

Ben started on the next screw, and after a lot of work, his fingers sore, he had taken the trap apart and freed two curved pieces of metal.

With a cry of effort, Ben kicked a toehold in the sticky surface and hoisted himself up, one gripping metal claw in each hand. He took another step, and then another, clasping the pit wall, never pausing, not daring to lose momentum, nor to lose his nerve; not allowing the slick surface time to crumble. With small stabbing movements, he got closer to the circle of light.

*Free us.*

The haunting images he'd seen rushed back into his head. *Who were those people?* He remembered the boy with long, dark hair; the small girl with the round, diseased face. What he'd seen and heard went through his mind as he climbed. It had all seemed so real. Ben felt his jaguar marks hot and uncomfortable as his arm scraped the soil. That girl's face; her ravaged skin. He jammed his toe into another foothold and swiped the metal claw. He couldn't get her out of his head.

Ben kicked another step into the pit wall, remembering what Yara had said. *They are the spirits of our people . . . forest people – our ancestors. . . Now their spirits haunt the jungle, yearning to be at peace.*

Well, Ben had seen them, he had felt them, and somehow he had been chosen to help them.

"*I can't give up!*" Ben told himself through gritted teeth as he pulled himself up.

The hole widened over him. Fireflies flew over it like floating embers. And with a last cry of pain he heaved himself over the lip of the pit and lay there panting, tasting soil, his heart beating wildly against the dark earth.

Ben rolled over on to his back and let out a long, slow gasp. He tried to collect his strength. *Get up! Get to camp!* he ordered himself, but his body felt so sore, so heavy, that he allowed himself a few more seconds of rest.

He had the sensation of something light touching the palm of his right hand. Then something crawled across the skin, and in a reflex he flicked his hand to get rid of whatever it was. There was a fluttering sensation over his knuckles: tickling, persistent.

There on his hand in the moonlight Ben saw a moth: a huge, bright yellow moth, with feathery antennae, and a dark eye pattern on each dusty wing. He moved his fingers and it rose into the air, dancing there for a few seconds before flitting away. He pulled himself up – and then there was a second one. Then another, and another.

Ben sat gaping, head tipped back. Now there was a mass of moths, hundreds of them, thousands, streaming by, like flakes of pale gold leaves carried on a river.

For a moment he was lost in the spectacular sight. What was it, a kind of migration? He knew some happened only under certain conditions; triggered by a change of temperature, for example, or by a full moon. The moths spiralled upwards, streaming together in one precise line. Ben found himself murmuring in wonder, then whispering the shaman's words: *follow the flying gold by moonlight. . .*

Ben felt his back stiffen; then he was scrabbling in his pocket for his compass, relieved to find it intact from the fall, hands shaking as he took the bearing of the moths streaming overhead.

They were all flying in exactly the same direction: *54° 35' west.*

He broke into a limping run, back along the moonlit trail, to Yara, to Raffie, his head buzzing. *Follow the flying gold by moonlight.* That was it! That was the way they must go next! He picked up speed, weaving his way along the track. That was the way to the Trial of the Howling Heights!

*Then by next nightfall must you complete your quest.*

He had one more day. Only *one more day* to find El Dorado and free Dad!

The light of the full moon gave the forest a ghostly

glow, and Ben felt the jaguar marks warm on his arm. He saw a thick snake slither quickly out of his way as he sprinted along the path, his feet strangely noiseless; the way strangely clear, despite the sinking moon; the sounds of the forest more acute in his ears. He smelt the sharp scent of the smouldering campfire, then saw its embers through the trees. Ben slowed down his pace, all his senses on alert.

He got to the edge of the clearing and stopped. Erskine and Luis were back; he could hear snores from inside their tents. But the flaps were closed and there was no sign of movement.

Stealthily, Ben crept to his friends' tent. Through the canvas he heard Raffie's low ragged breathing; Yara mumbling something quietly in her sleep. He slipped in and crept over to Raffie's bed, pulling open the mosquito net and shaking him awake.

Rafael stirred, his hammock wobbling. He swatted Ben's arm away, then twitched awake with a little gasp. Ben pressed a finger to his lips as Rafael's eyes widened and he fumbled to find his glasses. "What is it? What?"

"Shhh!" hissed Ben. "They mustn't hear us!"

Raffie got the glasses on and blinked through them in alarm. "Ben?"

Ben gestured Raffie to be quiet, then went over to wake Yara, who immediately sprang from her bed. "What is it?" she said, already seeming wide awake.

"We've got to get out." Ben grabbed a rucksack from the floor and started to stuff supplies into it. "And it has to be now."

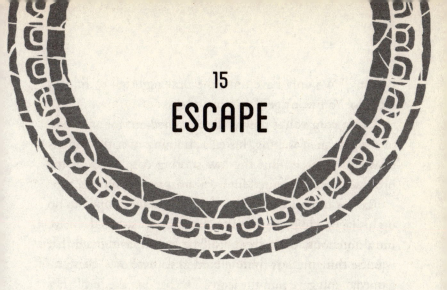

# 15
# ESCAPE

*"Our route will be from Dead Horse Camp, 11° 43'
south and 54° 35' west."*

COLONEL PERCY FAWCETT, 1925

"So that's the full story." Ben grabbed a water bottle and stuffed it into a rucksack. "We all fell for it; now we've just got to get out."

"How could Professor Erskine do that?" Yara whispered angrily as she pulled down a mosquito net and crammed it in the bag.

Raffie kept shaking his head sadly and whispering, "I don't believe it." He still looked gutted. "What if they come after us?" he hissed. "They'll hunt us down like they did that little jaguar!"

"Get your boots on!" Yara chided. "And you heard what

Ben said! We only have until the next nightfall to find El Dorado! You won't get far in just socks!

"Keep your voices down!" Ben listened out for any noise of the two men waking, his ears straining over the sounds of wailing insects. But the low snoring coming from the professor's tent reassured him – at least for the moment.

Raffie's mouth was a thin, tight line as he stooped to do up his laces. He looked as if he were about to cry. "He gave me a notebook for my research!" he wailed, as though that was the thing he was finding hardest to swallow. "Ben!" he gasped. "You gave him the icons! The bat *and* the bird!" His face flushed red. "He has no right! We've got to get them back!" He paced the tent, shoelaces dangling. "What if we need them, for the trials?"

"Raffie's right, Ben," said Yara. "We cannot leave without the icons."

"I know where he put them!" Rafael was already at the entrance to the tent. "Meet you by the trail!"

"Raffie!" hissed Ben – but before he could stop him, his friend was gone.

Ben forced his mind into gear. "We'll need more food with us, Yara, and more water. Luis keeps the supplies in a box by his tent – I'll go."

"I will find a machete!" said Yara.

Ben nodded. "Be fast." He pulled the rucksack on to his back as Yara disappeared into the shadows, and made his way towards Luis's tent. He saw the box of supplies just a few steps away, in the tent entrance.

But as he reached out for the lid, something moved

inside the tent and he stood rooted to the spot, hardly daring to breathe. The seconds felt like minutes. There was the hiss of a lamp, and a yellow glow flooded the inside. Through the gap in the tent flap, Ben saw Luis sat on an overturned bucket, his rifle across his lap. He was cleaning the barrel with an oily rag, in long, slow movements, whistling quietly.

Ben edged backwards. No way he could risk getting those supplies now. He found Yara waiting at the start of the track, staring wide-eyed at Luis's lit-up tent. Then he saw a figure moving quickly towards them and his heart skipped a beat – but it was Raffie who appeared, triumphantly holding up the gold bat and bird.

"Nice one, Raffie!" Ben mouthed, slipping them into the pouch with the spheres. "Now we've got to move."

"Got something else, too!" Rafael's eyes were glittering. He held up a book with a red cover: Professor Erskine's research book. "I'll teach him to mess with our heads!" he whispered. "And look, I got one of his maps as well!"

Ben gave him a thumbs-up. "Now *come on*!"

The moon was disappearing from view as they made their way along the track, its glow fading as the sky turned from black to ashy grey.

*First priority*, thought Ben: *put as many miles between us and the camp as possible. Secondly: head off on the compass bearing.*

When they seemed a safe distance he twisted on his head torch, and immediately insects swarmed towards the beam.

"Which way?" asked Yara, and he peered at the compass dial. Ben pointed a finger and she raised the machete, veering away from the track, making deft cuts through the tangled vegetation.

They pushed on, the brightening dawn streaking through the canopy and on to the forest floor. Ben paused to check the compass. *How long will we have to follow this bearing?* He took a turn with the machete. *How long before the professor and Luis come after us?* He felt his head glazed with sweat, but he still shivered.

"Five-minute rest, Ben?" called Yara. "I think Raffie has blisters."

They crouched in a pocket of daylight, sharing sips from the water canteen, Ben listening out for any sounds of their being followed, but hearing none.

Rafael took out Professor Erskine's thick research book and waggled it. "Maybe this will tell us what that cheat is up to!"

Ben flipped the book open.

On the first pages was a list of symbols: hieroglyphs, with notes about their meanings. He turned more pages. There were sketches and notes, all with sources and dates, some spanning right back.

"There's *years* of research there," Rafael grinned. "He'll be furious when he finds out we've taken it!" he added with relish.

"*The jaguar*," Ben read out, "*is revered as the most powerful of all the jungle creatures. . . He aids communication between the living and the dead. Of all the spirits, the most powerful is that of the jaguar.*

"*To clothe oneself as the jaguar,*" Ben continued, "*is to become the jaguar. . . All fabled rulers of El Dorado covered themselves in the fur of a jaguar.*"

"What?" exclaimed Rafael. "So Professor Erskine sees himself as some kind of ruler, do you think? Is that why he wants to dress up in a jaguar skin?"

Yara gave a quick nod. "And Ben," she said excitedly. "You said he was talking about a mask with Luis! Do you remember the inscription in the bat cave?"

"*He who wears the mask, wears the power of El Dorado,*" recited Ben. For some reason, the words still sent cold ripples along his spine.

"Is there anything about a mask in the book?" urged Rafael.

Ben flicked through the pages, scanning them. " Here," he said, after a while of searching. "Listen to this! *Without his face, the golden king is nothing. . .*'

"The golden king!" interrupted Yara. "I told you that our legend speaks of such a king – it is he who you must meet at the final trial Ben!"

"Wait!" said Ben. "Listen to the rest – there's stuff about the mask!" He rapidly carried on reading. "*The golden king was the god of the Ancients. In El Dorado a great temple was built to him. In a chamber at its very heart was placed his statue. . .* Ben took a breath. "Now, here's the bit. . ." His throat went dry as he read on. "*Legend says that when the MASK is replaced on the face of the golden king, his power will be restored, and he will welcome all lost spirits into the sanctuary of his city.*"

Rafael gave a little gasp.

"*Lost spirits,*" echoed Yara quietly. "The unquiet spirits." She looked at Ben, her eyes shining. 'That's how you will free them.'

Ben tried to take everything in. He had to find the temple, and place the mask back on the golden king's statue.

"And your Dad," said Yara. "He is lost somewhere inside that same spirit world. By freeing the spirits, you can free *him.*"

Ben leafed keenly through the book, but he couldn't find any more about the golden king or the mask. Instead, another piece of text caught his attention: what was it? A diary entry, a story? It was headed "*Amazon basin, 1960*".

"*The small boy watches the compass needle turn,*" Ben read – but before he could continue, Yara gripped his arm.

"Hear that?" she asked in a sharp whisper.

Ben listened. The noise was muffled at first, then became unmistakable – breaking twigs; footfalls. He sprang up, letting the book fall to the ground in his haste, pulling the others with him as the realization hit.

Professor Erskine and Luis were coming after them; tracking them down.

And they were gaining.

## Amazon basin, 1960

*The small boy watches the compass needle turn. He can't take his eyes off the small red arrow as it makes its slow rotations. He's fascinated. Confused. It shouldn't do that, should it? North is always north. South is always south. That's what Father taught him. Those were facts that you could depend on. Like Father and Mother. Constants. Safe things. Unchangeable things.*

*The compass point whirls faster.*

*The boy gazes out, at the bright blue sky. He has to screw up his eyes to look at it. Cloud, pulled into thin, tight wisps. He looks down from the small window. Green. Everywhere shadow green. Trees in every direction. Forest stretching as far as he can see.*

*The boy sees his father's hand tighten on the controls; sees him tap a dial and frowns, as he mutters something to Mother. They must have seen it too then, the spinning.*

*The plane flies closer to the rocks – rocks that catch the light like crystals. Pretty colours, patterns, holes. The engine growls, as the plane sweeps lower.*

*And at first it looks like smoke. . .*

*The boy presses his face hard against the window to see better. Black flows out from the rock crevasses in a flapping flood, each speck a bat.*

"Bank left!" the boy hears Father shout. He feels the plane tip sideways.

The sky goes dark with bats. They sweep up at them in a growing, spiralling mass. The plane rocks. Soft bodies thud against the glass like bullets. The boy jerks his head away as a bat hits the pane, leaving a web of cracks.

"More power!" He hears his mother's voice over the shuddering engine. "They'll damage the propeller!"

The plane lurches, drops. Shoulder straps bite the boy's shoulders as he is wrenched about inside his seat. Instinctively he leans forward, clamping his head between his knees, clenched fists raised round his head like a shield.

There is the scraping shriek of metal against rock. A grinding tearing. Sprays of sparks. . .

The small boy wanders from the crashed plane.

He knows they are dead. The way Father's body is twisted up inside the jagged metal of the cockpit. The way Mother's eyes are staring wide at nothing. The red across the throat.

He stumbles forward, upwards, not knowing where he's going, knowing only that he has to get away. Away from the smoke; away from the buckled metal and the blood.

On he climbs. But the light is too strong here. He has to shield his eyes from the dazzling glint ahead as he steps closer. And suddenly there is an outstretched hand. A face. Mouth open in a grimace. Pointed teeth. The small boy stares.

In front of him stands a man.

A man made of gold.

# 16
# WHISPERS

*"we went with fear and trembling into . . . the houses"*

MANUSCRIPT 512

No time to rest. The forest pressed in from all sides as Ben cut a way through with the machete. The canopy was thick here, blocking most of the sunlight. He had the compass round his neck, and now and again he stopped to squint at the bearing, listening for their pursuers.

Ben felt sweat trickle into his eyes and a queasy feeling grip his stomach, but he kept up the punishing pace. He mistimed a machete blow and staggered, falling heavily, landing only centimetres from the blade.

"Are you all right, Ben?" Yara panted, frowning. "Raffie – you are limping!"

"Just my blisters," Rafael wheezed. "Of course, they could

easily go septic and I lose the foot – but we can't slow down! Luis is a trained killer; he tracks live prey for a living."

"My turn to carry the bag at least, Raffie," she said, tugged at the straps of the backpack.

They slogged on, Ben at the front, hacking into the dense forest, Yara watchful at the back.

"It's difficult to breathe," Raffie hobbled forward, and Ben saw that his friend's pace was getting slower and slower.

"It's the humidity," Ben said, wiping perspiration from his hot face. A low growl of thunder echoed ahead of them. "It'll get less when the rain comes," he said encouragingly.

Yara nodded, snatching handfuls of leaves and plucking vegetation from the forest floor as she followed. Whatever she was doing had a purpose, but Ben decided not to waste his breath asking unnecessary questions.

"We have to keep going, Raffie," he said, striding forward – and then all of a sudden he broke out through the trees into some kind of clearing, open to the dense grey sky. The space took him so much by surprise so that he almost lost his balance.

In front of them was an overgrown collection of huts, and the children stood close together, taking in the scene.

The huts' thatched roofs were half caved-in; vines snaked up bamboo walls with gaping holes. Ben cautiously moved from building to building, but there was no sign of life.

"Raffie needs to rest, Ben!" Yara insisted, gazing around her with a nervous look. "I want to treat the sores on his feet."

"I'm OK," mumbled Rafael, but Ben could see that his friend could hardly stand up.

"We'll stop here for a bit, then," Ben said. "But we can't risk staying too long."

He cocked his head to listen; the drone of insects was suddenly obliterated by the curtain of rain that fell and drenched them in seconds. Seeing Raffie stumble, Ben grabbed him and with Yara's help pulled him into the darkness of a long-abandoned hut. They ducked through the low doorway and sank on to the dirt floor.

Ben wrinkled his nose. The inside of the hut was filled with the smell of earth, decay. It was as if something died in there.

The three of them sat huddled as they stared round. Stones circled the black ashes of a fire pit; otherwise the room was completely empty.

"Who lived in this village?" whispered Rafael as rain dripped through holes in the roof. "Why did they abandon this place?"

Yara was pale. "I do not know, but it feels as if bad things happened here."

After a few seconds pause, Ben saw her shake herself into action. She chose a flat stone from the edge of the fire pit, then tore pieces of the leaves she had collected on to it and began to grind them with another of the stones. She cupped her hand to collect water from the leaking roof, then added drops to the mixture, and Ben watched as she worked everything into a thick paste. "Boots and socks off, Rafael!" she ordered.

Ben offered round the water bottle, then put it under a leak in the roof to refill it. He opened their only packet of biscuits and rationed out one each. His sense of unease was growing. "As soon as the rain stops, we get moving again."

He unrolled the map Rafael had taken from the professor. "But first, I want to check where we're heading."

Ben found the bluff where they'd camped, and plotted their course with the compass. "*Thermal area. Unstable ground*," he read. "That's where we'll be soon; then we'll be totally off the map."

"Like the brave explorers in the olden days," said Rafael, wincing as he pulled off his sock. "I'm descended from a conquistador, as you know."

"That's nothing to be proud of!" Yara told him. "Now, let me hold your foot. Stop wiggling your toes!"

"Are you sure you got the ingredients right?" grimaced Rafael. "There are a lot of deadly poisonous plants that look very similar."

"Be quiet, Rafael!" Yara scooped paste from the stone. "This will hurt a lot," she told him, then smeared it quickly over his blisters.

Rafael yelped and broke into a stream of Portuguese.

Yara wasn't letting up. "Your brave explorers of the olden days stole our country's precious things!" she said sharply. "And they brought diseases with them that killed thousands of our people."

Ben shakily hung the compass back round his neck. He remembered the visions he had seen: the boy with long, dark hair and the melting gold; the little girl with the round face covered in those terrible welts. He looked into the fire pit, suddenly not able to draw his eyes away. His arm throbbed and when he rubbed the skin he felt his four scars, raised up and tender to the touch. Yara's voice faded into the background as he stared into the dead ashes.

Without warning, Ben saw the room fill with creeping shadows as little tongues of gold flame sprang from the blackened fire pit. They crackled and spat. From far away came the sound of voices. . . And suddenly the space was full of figures; people sitting round the fire. . .

*There are voices.*

*Echoes from somewhere far away. Far back.*

They want to take us from our homes, *comes a voice that is many voices.*

*Men shout from outside the hut; then the walls are alight, flames licking up to the ceiling of the hut. There are people running, gunshots.*

*A mother clutches her screaming baby, their wide eyes lit by fire. The baby claws at his mother, and her face is lined with a desperate anguish.*

*A strange whisper lingers in the air. A whisper that is many whispers.*

*Help us! Find El Dorado.*

*Restore the golden king's power.*

*Give us back our home.*

*Free us.*

And as soon as it had come, the vision was gone. Ben sat

in a daze. ". . .and they murdered whole families in their homes," he heard Yara tell Rafael angrily, as she smeared his foot with the ointment. "Those are the kind of conquistador people *you* are descended from!"

"I am *not*!" Rafael bit his bottom lip.

"The past is our present," Yara snapped, slapping more ointment on to Rafael's foot. "Blame is passed on until redemption."

*There it is again*, thought Ben. He swallowed hard as he recovered from the shock of images. That word *redemption* – the shaman had used it too.

"You can't blame me for what my ancestors did. Can she, Ben? Ben?" The anger drained out of Rafael's voice as he peered at his friend's face.

"What is it, Ben?" said Yara, her forehead creased with concern, and she and Rafael listened wide-eyed as Ben told them about his vision.

"The unquiet spirits really need their new home," said Rafael quietly, after Ben had finished. "But why El Dorado?" he said. "Why is it the only place they can go to find peace?"

"It is the only place they can feel safe?" suggested Yara. "Under the protection of the golden king?"

The rain had stopped. The sun had come out again and felt hot through the broken bamboo slats.

Ben had a sudden painful longing to see his dad, twisted together with self-doubt. "But will we ever find El Dorado?"

"Yes," Yara told him firmly. "My grandfather believes in you and I believe in you as well."

"Me too," said Raffie earnestly, pulling on his socks. He

nodded his head so much that his glasses nearly fell off. "If anyone can do it, you can Ben!"

"Thanks, guys," said Ben quietly. "I'll try my best. Now we've got to get moving. If we're lucky, the heavy rain will have covered our tracks. You OK to walk, Raffie?"

Rafael laced up his boots. "Thanks to Yara."

On they went, following the compass. They were climbing now and the forest thinned, giving less shade from the sun as it belted down. They took rests, sipped water, chewed on the last of the biscuits to keep their energy levels up.

Ben began to worry more and more. They were leaving the forest behind completely. *How can that fit with the clue about a forest?*

The compass led them ever upwards and the ground got steeper, the vegetation sparser, until they were walking on mainly rock.

They hiked on, Ben not daring to slacken the pace. Rock pinnacles towered ahead of them. Underfoot the rocks were sunk into reddish soil, and there were other colours now too: rainbows of mud under their boots.

Ben stopped. "Smell that?" It was like something rotting. Bad eggs.

"Hydrogen sulphide," said Raffie, wrinkling his nose. From somewhere ahead of them came a strange low hiss: an eerie rushing of air. Ben was reminded of waves rushing up a pebble beach.

Ben felt Rafael press close to his shoulder.

The noise got louder; increased to a wail, then a howling.

But as soon as it had come, the noise was gone.

"Monkeys?" said Ben, though it didn't sound like monkeys he'd ever heard. "Or another kind of animal?"

Yara shook her head. "I have never heard animals make a sound like that."

They continued more cautiously, and as they reached the top of the section, the valley opened out and they drew to an abrupt stop.

The space was flanked on both sides by high, sheer cliffs, and between these cliffs was a series of terraces of all colours, like wide, low steps, patterned in places with thin cracks from which wispy white vapour was escaping.

Rising up from the terraces were pale towers of rock like melted candles, fat at the bottom, tapering to rounded points, and thick creepers trailing over the cliff edges had found their way across the space, latching on to the tops of the towers; a bizarre cat's cradle strung overhead.

"Beautiful," whispered Yara.

And what was that at the very top of the terraces? Ben shielded his eyes from the glare of the sun. Some kind of stunted tree? It was difficult to make out. Branches stuck out at all angles, with pointed leaves along them.

"The terraces and towers are all made of minerals," gasped Rafael. "Crystal deposits. It must be that area marked on the map, remember – the part that was marked unstable ground?"

"Well, the compass takes us right through it," said Ben, double-checking the dial. "And I can't see any way round, can you?" He pressed the tip of his boot cautiously on to the edge of the first terrace: a smooth, pale gold surface with flecks of pink. "I'll go first." He let the ground take his weight. He heard the delicate crystals crunch under his sole, but the ground seemed firm enough.

"Be careful," said Rafael, as he and Yara followed.

It was only a small step up on to the next terrace. This time the surface was a shining cream colour, with ribbons of turquoise and goldish specks running through it. Lines of cool shadows criss-crossed the surface from the overhead creepers.

Ben felt more confident with every step. As he went up on to the third step – a pale red shelf with a surface of shining turquoise crystals – he was even starting to enjoy the sensation of walking on the terraces. His front boot pressed confidently on to the deposit – but then he immediately felt it give. He heard the snapping of crystals as his boot broke the brittle crust. He drew back sharply with a gasp, pivoting himself on to his back foot as the surface ahead of him crumbled – to leave a gaping hole filled with boiling water.

Ben flung out an arm. "Stop!" And he himself stopped so abruptly that Raffie ran into the back of him, making Ben stagger forward to the very edge.

They stood staring at the hole, bubbling like a witch's cauldron: scorching and lethal. Ben's heart sank as he gazed up the terraces. There was still such a long way to go. How would they know which ground was stable and which wasn't?

And then Ben heard it. That same hissing rush of air

they'd heard from lower down the valley. He felt the ground tremble. The hiss rose to a sinister wail, then to a howl. It was deafening, terrifying, echoing off the rocks so it seemed to be coming from every direction at once. Ben felt his whole body tense. He was unable to move. But something was coming, he felt it . . . heading straight for them.

# 17
# THE TRIAL OF THE HOWLING HEIGHTS

A howling plume of water shot from the ground, only metres from where they were standing, gushing high into the air.

Ben lurched back, pulling Yara and Raffie with him, as scalding water rained down. He felt a drop splash on to his hand, burning the skin.

"Geyser!" Raffie wheezed, once they were out of range.

Ben hardly had time to catch his breath before a second geyser erupted from a terrace further up, and as that one started to lose height and power, a third hurtled skywards from another spot, each in rapid succession. Faster than high-power fire hoses. Boiling towers of hissing water spat steam in all directions.

*Could it be?* Shakily, excited, Ben pulled out the gold bird icon and looked at the clue on the back. It fitted, didn't it? What if the lines with spiralling tops didn't represent trees in a forest at all? Instead what if they were a picture of these deadly geysers?

"Howling heights!" shouted Yara over the wail of the water, as there was a fourth, then a fifth steaming column.

The geysers died down and the ground was still again. Everything went eerily quiet.

"So." Ben wet his lips. A mixture of excitement and fear swept through him. "Looks like we've found the next trial."

"Geysers are superheated water under pressure," Raffie stuttered, still trembling after their near miss. "They are instant death for anyone who gets in their way."

"Should be a doddle to deal with, then," said Ben.

So how *would* they ever pass? One foot wrong on the fragile ground and they'd plunge into scalding water, and even if they found stable ground, a geyser could erupt under them at any second.

For a moment, the situation felt hopeless. But there must be a way to pass the trial, Ben's inner voice reasoned, however impossible it seemed.

"How are we ever going to reach the top, Ben?" Yara asked. "Make a dash for it when the geysers have stopped?"

As they stood there thinking, the wailing started again, and they watched as the succession of geysers performed their deadly show.

"Not enough time, Yara," shouted Ben over the roar.

Part-way through the spectacle, Ben felt Rafael grip his arm. He jiggled Ben's elbow up and down, face looking like he was bursting to tell Ben something. "They can be timed!" he mouthed.

"What do you mean?" yelled Ben as another geyser burst into life.

"Like Old Faithful in Yellowstone National Park!" said Rafael excitedly. "I went there once. You can set your clock by that geyser!"

Ben nodded as he began to understand what Rafael was getting at.

"Remember the games of chess we played on the boat?" Rafael went on. "You make a move, then the geysers make a move." Rafael pulled up his sleeve to look at his watch. "This trial's all about strategy, surely!"

Ben got it! They'd be able to time the jets; predict when the next one was coming. "Raffie – you're a genius!"

"Then there's the problem of the unstable ground. . ." Rafael paced about a bit and then stopped and clicked his fingers. "That's linked to the *colours* of the crystals – must be!

"Is it?" asked Yara.

Rafael hopped about, his eyes bright. "Those reddish patches, we know we have to stay off those, but the parts with any kind of gold specks, I think they contain pyrite – fool's gold, people used to call it – and those deposits are thick and can take our weight."

"Awesome!" exclaimed Yara. She scanned up the terraces. "Some of the gold areas are pretty far apart, though," in a much less certain tone.

Ben squinted up the terraces, tracking the safe, gold-specked patches between where they were standing and that strange-looking tree at the top. There were several; but it wasn't exactly going to be easy. He gulped. In places they'd need to take a good few staggering jumps and break a few Olympic records on the way.

*Unless. . .*

Ben looked up at the creepers strung overhead between the rock towers, then pulled at a stem and it came down like a rope. He tugged the vine to see if it was strong enough, then eased himself up so that his whole weight was suspended. It swayed and creaked unnervingly – but it held.

"OK." Ben let go of the creeper and wiped his forehead. "Do you see what we have to do?"

"I do!" said Yara. "Let me practise!" She took a running leap on to the creeper, swinging several metres over an unstable area before landing deftly on firm ground.

"What? We need to use the creepers to get across the gaps?" Raffie looked petrified, but then he nodded. "I don't usually do swinging, but . . . I'll try."

Ben saw Yara give Rafael's shoulder a reassuring squeeze. He scrutinized his watch. "Right, now we need to memorize the geyser pattern."

Rafael flipped open his notebook and chewed the end of his pen and they waited for the geysers to start again. The hissing rose to a wail, then crescendoed into a howl.

"Here it comes!" Ben yelled. "Concentrate, everyone!"

The first geyser sprang into action and then the other jets performed. When the spectacle was over, the three of them used Raffie's scribbles to fine-tune the sequence.

"Five seconds here, then pause for three, then swing *here*, then jump *here*. . ." Rafael made sweeping arrows across the page, as if he was a coach going through the moves in a football game. "Got it?"

"I'll go first," said Ben, wriggling out of his rucksack and hiding it behind a rock. He couldn't afford that extra weight, but he didn't want it to be obvious that they'd been this way. "I'll test out getting across and pull the creepers into position. You two can come across on another sequence and. . ." He stopped speaking.

A faint, high-pitched sound was coming from somewhere behind them – and it wasn't the geysers.

Yara spun round. "There is only one person who whistles like that!" she said.

"The Professor and Luis have tracked us down!" cried Rafael, his face pale. "We can't have more than few minutes until they get here!"

"We have to go across *now*. All of us!" Ben took one last glance at the notes, then snapped the book shut and shoved it back at Rafael. "Follow my moves!" He just had to hope he had the pattern memorized correctly.

Already the hissing of a geyser had started up again, getting louder by the second.

"Keep the timings precise," Ben muttered to himself. "Wait, then move fast."

His friends were depending on him to lead them safely across.

The ground vibrated under Ben's feet as the pressure started to build. There'd be only one chance, he told himself. Only time for one crossing before Luis and the professor arrived – if that.

The ominous wailing below ground turned into a howl.

"Go!" Heart lurching, Ben darted forward, leaping from

161

one patch of gold-specked ground to the next, crunching down on the solid layers of pyrite.

"Five seconds, three steps right. . ." He shouted instructions to himself as he went. "Pause for three!"

He stopped for a moment on the stable ground, timing his next move, then sprang to catch hold of a creeper to give him momentum.

He heard the gush of the first geyser behind him, felt the rush of steamy heat in the air as he dodged between the rock pillars, glancing back to check his friends were close behind.

The soles of his boots went tacky with the heat from the ground; sweat ran down his face. *Know when to move; know when to pause.* But it was hard to be patient when he thought about the chambers of superheated water right under him. "Now!" he yelled. "*Now!*"

They were more than halfway across when it happened.

Ben was holding on to a rock tower, timing his next move, when he heard a scream. He twisted to look behind him and gave a cry of shock: both Rafael and Yara were stranded, the terrace collapsing in a wide radius round them, water bubbling visciously on all sides.

And there was less than a minute until the next geyser blew.

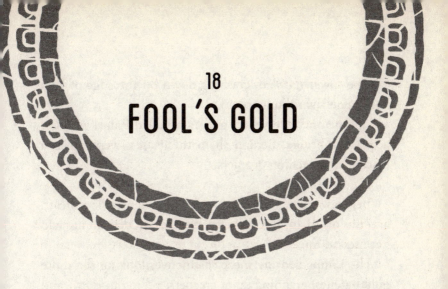

# 18
# FOOL'S GOLD

Had a creeper broken? Had a leap been mistimed? *No time to think about that now*, Ben told himself – *help them!*

There were no vines within reach, and in any case the gap was too wide to swing across without a massive run-up and he had no space for that.

With maybe only half a minute left, only one thing came into his head.

Ben got behind the rock tower and rammed it with his shoulder as hard as he could. He ignored the jarring pain and crashed against it again. He let his torso smack into the rock a third time, and felt the tower give a little.

He kicked the base viciously with his foot, then battered against it again, then again. He felt the ground quake under him with the building pressure; saw steam fizz along the geyser fissure as the seconds ticked down.

There was a loud *snap* and the tower teetered. With a shout, Ben slammed forward with his whole body.

The tower toppled, crashing down on the edge of Yara and Rafael's shrinking island.

"Come on!" Ben yelled, and Yara pulled Rafael with her across the bridge. Behind them the geyser swept up in a cascade of scorching droplets.

*Go. Go. Go!*

Ben saw them get safely across and then took a breath and was off again. But the delay now meant the timings had got messed up.

His jumps became more instinctive; looking for those gold patches; grabbing up at creepers; yelling to Raffie and Yara over the terrible din of the geysers. The other side loomed close, the strange tree at the top of the terraces alluringly near. A strange confidence surged through his body, similar to what he'd felt when he'd climbed like a bat; dived like a bird. He made a series of wild, bounding strides, pulling the others along with him.

With a final graceful leap he sprang . . . and landed, feeling the crust breaking under his back heel and a spray of scalding water. He spun round to wrench his friends towards him, and the three of them collapsed in a heap behind the tree.

It was a while before any of them could speak.

"Thanks, Ben," Yara said at last.

Raffie's chest was heaving like a piston. "Can you see anyone coming?" he rasped. "They won't be able to follow us across the geysers, will they?"

Ben peered out from behind the trunk and down the terraces. There might have been a movement – it was difficult to tell through the thick steam. "Let's not stick around to find out."

As Ben stood, he realized with a start that the tree they were behind was not a tree at all. What he'd thought were branches were actually twisting limbs of rock; its leaves were really diamond-shaped crystals that glinted in a myriad of colours. What had seemed to be the bark was rainbow swirls of minerals.

It was an ancient-looking rock formation, and when Ben looked closely he could make out a frame of hieroglyphs, like the ones he'd seen carved in the bat cave and round the hole where he'd found the bird. When he pressed firmly at the surface inside the frame, the deposits fell away to reveal an exactly square opening.

He heard Rafael gasp.

"Awesome!" exclaimed Yara.

Ben reached in and took out an alabaster box, identical to the first two, and held it out to Yara. "Go on," he said, holding it out to her. "Your turn."

Yara gave a smile. "Any guesses what's inside?" She slipped the catch and lifted the lid.

"A monkey!" she said in delight, reaching forward to stroke its gleaming surface.

Ben nodded. The Trial of the Howling Heights had needed speed, agility, cleverness, daring, balance – what better than a monkey!

He took the icon out of the box and turned it over, and his friends crowded in close to see. . .

But the back surface was blank; completely smooth.

"But we don't need a clue this time, do we?" said Rafael. He pointed ahead of them, and Ben saw how the top terrace they were on continued, narrowing to pass between high cliffs, and becoming a rocky gully which climbed out of sight. It was the only way forward. And the ground through the narrow valley – he let out a long breath – it was paved with wide, smooth stones.

"It's a road!" Ben cried. "Someone built a road through here! Come on!"

They hurried up the slender canyon, following the ancient road. As they got higher, the cliffs became dotted with sparkling crystals.

"We must be getting close now, Ben, don't you think?" He heard the anticipation in Rafael's voice, together with a wobble of fear.

"I am sure we must be," said Yara.

Up they climbed, but as time passed there was still no sight of the end. It was thirsty work without water, and they'd eaten their last biscuit long before. Storm clouds gathered, and a strange, cold wind started blowing that made Ben shiver.

Rafael pressed close alongside, looking worried. "What will the next trial involve, Ben, do you think? Will the guardians of the dead really be dead?"

On they went, stumbling over the loose rocks of the path, sending scatterings of stones bouncing back down the slope. Their pace was definitely getting slower. Now above them was a constant mass of swirling clouds, with only brief glimpses of the sun.

Every time Ben thought they were about to reach the top, they crested the brow and another, even steeper slope stretched up ahead of them. And it was while they were resting on one of these ridges that Yara suddenly gave a frightened cry, pointing back the way they'd come.

Ben followed her outstretched finger to see two figures below them, moving fast up through the gully.

*The professor. Luis.*

"But how did they get past the geysers?" Rafael looked stunned.

Ben scrambled to his feet. *How had they?*

"The crystals we crushed as we went across!" exclaimed Yara. "They must have seen where we stepped and timed the geysers like we did, and followed our footsteps—"

There was an ear-splitting crack – a gun being fired into the air.

"Come on!" shouted Ben. His mind went into overdrive as they rushed on.

*Can we hide?* There were no hiding places, only the smooth, sheer walls of the gully.

*Can we set a trap?* Ben scoured the ground for some kind of weapon; even scooped up a jagged rock from the ground. But then he let it fall. What use would a stone be against a gun?

They pushed the pace still further. Ben's throat was sore when he swallowed. He stumbled, nearly spraining his ankle on the uneven roadway. Luis's creepy whistling echoed up the canyon walls, alternating between getting louder, and then fainter.

They reached a twist in the gully, finding a trickle of water coming down the rock.

"Got to drink!" said Ben, and they took brief turns, Ben lapping fast like an animal, feeling energy filter through his aching muscles.

The ground was different here, he noticed, as he drew away from the rock wiping his mouth. A soft, reddish mud, with a metallic salty smell, like the tang of blood.

"Lots of iron round here," Raffie muttered, glancing nervously behind them. "Can we go now please?"

They were about to leave, but Yara suddenly pointed at the compass round Ben's neck. "Look what it is doing!" she cried.

Ben watched the needle spin, round and round, refusing to settle. . .

But before he could think what to make of it, there was the deafening crack and crystals shattered and ricocheted off the rock right by them.

Ben instinctively dived for the ground, flattening himself against it, and saw Yara and Raffie do the same. Another shot. A bullet whizzed over their heads.

"Up! Go!" Keeping low, they stumbled towards where the gully turned out of sight, Ben's thoughts going hyper as he braced himself for more shots. *Get out of range!*

They pushed on, rounding the bend. . . And there was something up ahead of them, catching the light – something metallic?

Ben came to an abrupt stop and bent to catch his breath. He wiped the sweat from his eyes, hardly believing what he was seeing.

The shattered wings. The mangled propeller.

In front of them was a wreck: the twisted, rusted fuselage of a crashed plane, pinned between the two sides of the gully walls, completely blocking their way.

And pressed against the smashed front window of the cockpit was a human skull.

# 19
# VALLEY OF SHADOWS

A skull. Jaw hanging open. Shattered bone.

Ben took a shaky step forward, trying to take in the scene. As he approached the smashed plane window he saw that there was another body, a second sun-bleached skeleton, twisted over the plane's controls.

"They are Professor Erskine's parents." Yara was by his shoulder, speaking in a shocked whisper. "They must be, must they not?"

Rafael couldn't take his eyes off the bones. "We've got to get past," he said, gripping the sides of his glasses. "Before they come with the gun."

Ben looked back at the plane, seeing the way its underbelly and smashed wing stubs lay like a barrier before them. There was no way round. No way under. He stared through the mangled hole where the cabin door had once been, seeing a slit of daylight showing beyond. "Let me check if there's a way through." He quickly approached the doorway and, wary of the jagged metal edges, levered himself up and inside, into the chaos of metal and wires and strewn objects.

"Hurry!" Yara urged.

And now Ben saw the tear in the other side of the fuselage. Their escape route. "We can get through!" he shouted. "Climb up!"

As he turned back to help the others he tripped on something and nearly went sprawling. It was some kind of half-decayed travel bag, the old-fashioned kind. His eye caught a brass nameplate on it and, seized with curiosity, he stooped to wipe away its film of grime.

*PETER. . .*

Ben peered at the tarnished metal.

*PETER and PENELOPE ERSKINE*

Ben let out a breath. So that confirmed it. Yara was right. These were Professor Erskine's explorer parents. Erskine *had* been here as a boy. The stories about him were all true.

In that claustrophobic, derelict space, Ben had a sudden image of Erskine as a tiny boy, the only survivor of the crash, alone in this remote place with the bodies of the two dead parents he'd seen killed. What might that do to someone, to a child – to their head? Suddenly he felt sorry for the professor. He knew himself what it was like to lose a mum, a dad. . .

"Hurry up! Come inside!" Ben called again to the others. What was taking them so long?

There was a noise behind him, breathing, and he turned. "You were right, Yara—"

But it wasn't Yara who appeared through the doorway. Nor Raffie.

It was Professor Erskine.

One look at Erskine's face was all it took. In an instant Ben's pity evaporated.

"Where is the gold you stole from me?"

Ben instinctively slipped a hand into the pocket where the three icons were nestled inside the pouch with the stones, closing his fingers round it protectively.

Erskine was a sight. He was no longer the smart and tidy explorer Ben had first met. His hair was ruffled and his clothes were streaked with dirt.

Behind he saw Luis, his rifle raised, his gaunt features difficult to read.

Erskine reached in through the doorway and gripped the collar of Ben's shirt, pulling him out and down to the ground.

"I didn't steal anything!" Ben gripped the icons inside a fist. "*You're* the thief!"

"And a liar!" shouted Raffie bravely.

Erskine's hand was still round Ben's throat – but the man wasn't going to get the gold icons off him, no way! He'd fight for them if he had to!

Yara and Raffie started forward, but Luis swung his rifle in their direction and they stopped in their tracks.

"You tried to kill us!" Yara's face was pale.

Luis gave an arrogant grin. "Do you think I would have missed, unless I'd wanted to?"

"Enough wasting time – I saw the moths' migration

as well, Jaguar Boy. I made the connection. I know we only have until nightfall! Now give me the icons!" Erskine snatched at Ben's pocket and in the scuffle that followed, the strap round Ben's neck got snapped and the compass fell.

Erskine let go and Ben fell back hard, then scrambled over to his friends, eyeing the gun and watching the professor.

Erskine bent to the ground, then slowly lifted the compass, gazing at the needle as if mesmerized.

Ben could see that it was still spinning rapidly.

Raffie nudged Ben with his elbow. "I worked it out!" he whispered, not taking his eyes off Erskine. "It's all the magnetic iron in the rock. This whole mountainside looks like it's made of it! Sends the compass mad."

Erskine looked up from the compass at the crashed plane, as if the memories of what had happened were only just coming back to him. "North should always be north," he muttered to himself. "South should always be south. Those are facts one can depend on."

Ben exchanged looks with Yara and Rafael.

Erskine pointed at one of the deep fissures in the rock gully. "That's where they flew out from! They got into our engines." Erskine screened his eyes as he stared up into the sky, at the clouds pulled into thick wisps. "There were bats everywhere!"

*Bats?* Ben thought. Had Erskine totally flipped? Even Luis had lowered his rifle a fraction and his eyes narrowed. He seemed to be watching the professor's every movement.

And it was only at that moment that Ben registered what was on Luis's back, rolled up and strapped to the hunter's pack.

He felt his stomach twist.

An animal skin.

A black jaguar skin.

*My jaguar.*

He gaped. *But how?* He'd destroyed all the traps; triggered the pit. Then he remembered with a jolt of shock – the very first trap he'd seen Luis with. There had been *five* traps, not four. *How can you have been so stupid?*

The enormity of it hit Ben then. The majestic head; the intelligent-looking face. Saving the animal from the rapids; releasing the jaguar from its cage. . . What he had felt when the jaguar first looked at him.

An unbearable pain rippled through the wounds on Ben's arm. He stumbled forward a few steps. He saw the symmetry of the dark diamonds between the empty eye sockets. It was as if a piece of himself was roped on to that pack.

"You killed the jaguar!" Ben's shock turned to raw anger. "That's the jaguar I freed! You had no right!"

Erskine ignored him. He appeared not even to hear what Ben said. The man stared at the crashed plane, as if seeing it for the first time. Then he strode past Ben, over to the wreckage, and went inside.

Through the front windscreen, Ben watched as Erskine reached the cockpit. The man hesitated and then started pulling manically at the front panels, wrenching at the controls to free one of the bodies, ripping away debris, peeling off the metal as if they were sheets of dead skin.

"What's he doing?" Raffie whimpered.

"He is truly out of his mind," whispered Yara.

All three children stood rooted to the spot. It was alarming to watch. Erskine was calling out as he worked, the same word, over and over. "Father! Father!"

When he came back out, he was holding a skull.

Raffie gave a frightened hiccup.

Ben stared. Erskine was cradling the skull in his two hands. The professor ran a finger, almost lovingly, around the empty eye sockets.

Again Ben felt that same stab of pity. "I'm sorry," he said quietly, "about your parents."

Erskine looked right at him. Fixed him with a cold stare. Then he raised the skull above his head, and flung it hard against the gully wall.

Ben and his friends gasped. Shards of bone and fragments of rock flew in all directions.

Then Erskine turned to them. "You want to know how I survived while my parents didn't?" he challenged, looming over them. "There wasn't a single mark on me." Ben saw that he was almost smiling; it was stomach-turning to see. "Not a cut; not a bruise; not one mark. How do you explain that?" he demanded.

"Good seat-belt straps?" suggested Rafael shakily. "The angle of the impact?"

"Because I was *chosen*!" Erskine retorted. "I was the first human to find my way to the gate of El Dorado since the Ancients closed the way."

"Who do you think you are?" asked Yara contemptuously. "Some kind of god?"

At these words, Erskine broke into a real smile. It was a grotesque sight.

Ben glanced at Luis, whose rifle was still directed at them. It was impossible to know what he was thinking.

"That's why I was led there," Erskine ranted on, "and shown its gateway as a boy. That's why the jaguar spirit led me to safety, until the right time came for me to enter the City."

"But you killed the jaguar!" It was Ben's turn to shout now. "It helped you when you were a child, and you killed it!"

"You really have no idea, Jaguar Boy, do you. . ." – Erskine looked at Ben pityingly – "what lies behind the gate."

"I know about the temple!" said Ben. "And the golden king's mask!"

"We read your research!" Rafael cried. "Or was it research you stole from other people you murdered?"

"And what else do you know?" Erskine asked quietly. He went to Luis and tugged at the straps of the pack, taking off the jaguar skin and unfurling it.

Dry-mouthed, Ben remembered words from Erskine's research book: *Of all the spirits, the most powerful is that of the jaguar. . . To clothe oneself as the jaguar is to become the jaguar. . .*

The pelt unfurled down Erskine's back, the head with the empty eye sockets over his skull like a weird kind of crown, bared fangs covering his forehead.

Raffie let out a nervy giggle, but Erskine silenced him with a look. "When I enter El Dorado and wear the golden king's mask, my transformation will be complete."

Ben stared. Erskine seemed different now he was wearing the skin. Taller – stronger, somehow. What would happen if he got to wear the mask as well?

That didn't bear thinking about.

"The mask has to stay in El Dorado," Ben said hotly. "On the face of the true golden king."

"Yes!" cried Yara with passion. "Or the unquiet spirits can never be free!"

"What do I care about the spirits?" scoffed Erskine. "What are they compared with the power that wearing the king's mask will bring me?"

*He who wears the mask* . . . the words shunted again through Ben's mind . . . *wears the power of El Dorado.*

Briefly, Ben's eyes caught Luis's, but the hunter's face remained distant, unreadable.

"Move!" With a nod from Erskine, Luis was forcing them on, the rifle at their backs. One by one they climbed up into the plane's ruined cabin and lowered themselves through the tear in the fuselage, then out through the other side.

They were frog-marched on, Ben in a daze as he led the group up the steepening slope. Whatever happened, he knew this much: they had to stop Erskine from getting the mask.

On they climbed. The eerie silence was broken only by the wind whispering in the rock gullies above them, and the sound of their breathing.

They headed into low cloud, and through its clammy mist, then broke out into unexpectedly bright afternoon sunlight.

Ben stopped, blinking in the glare. Ahead of him was a man's shape, motionless, facing him as they came up the gully.

*Dad?* Could it be?

He broke into a stumbling upward run, not caring about Luis's rifle, not caring about the professor's angry shouts, just hoping while not daring to, his heart thudding. "They've got a gun!" he shouted. "Dad!"

But as he approached, he slowed down. The figure didn't look so much like Dad any more. It's face reflected the sun straight into his eyes, and he had to shield them from the dazzling glint as he stepped closer.

He reached the end of the gully, and a sheer wall of rock, and came face to face with not one man, but two.

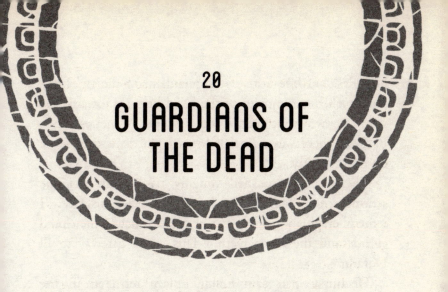

# 20
# GUARDIANS OF
# THE DEAD

*"The view was so beautiful that none could take their eyes from their reflections."*

MANUSCRIPT 512

Two stone men, their faces painted gold. Ben stared at the tall sculptures, each half-embedded in the towering cliff that barred the way. They were so real-looking, he expected their eyes to snap open at any moment and the men to start breathing. Instead their lids stayed closed as if they were asleep. The only part of their devilish faces that wasn't gold was their teeth, which were sharp white and bared – more animal than human.

"*The guardians of the dead*," Yara whispered by Ben's shoulder.

The guardian on the left had his arms straight against

his sides, but one arm of the guardian on the right was outstretched – the palm of the hand held up towards the sky. The two stone men stood a couple of metres apart. Between them was a line of hieroglyphs, as if over some unseen doorway.

The professor pushed roughly past to inspect the sentinels, and Ben felt the jaguar fur brush his face. "I remember: this was the place." Erskine touched the closed eyelids and the sharp teeth. "This is the gateway to El Dorado!"

Fleetingly Ben saw Erskine's face reflected in the demonic face.

The professor stood back and folded his arms. "Find the way through, then, Jaguar Boy," he challenged. "Show us what you were chosen to do."

"Careful, Ben!" warned Rafael, shuffling back a little. "It's bound to be booby-trapped!"

'I'm doing this for Dad,' Ben said, stepping forward, giving Erskine a defiant look. "And the unquiet spirits. Not you."

He tentatively pressed a hand on to the rock face between the guardians, then ran his fingers quickly over the smooth surface.

*There was going to be a secret lever, right? Like you saw in the films. Something to press or twist, maybe.*

Ben continued to explore, but there was no sign of anything other than the solid wall. He turned his attention to the guardians, and they were unexpectedly cold under his touch.

Ben glanced at Luis, and saw the rifle still levelled at his friends. Erskine stood there watching him closely, but keeping a distance.

*What are you afraid of, Erskine?* Ben felt wisps of mist cool his face as he continued his search. There had to be something! Shadows grew and shrank over the stone. The sun dropped a little lower, deepening the gloom.

But Ben still had no clue how to open the doorway.

"The hieroglyphs. . ." he heard the Professor say, and Ben turned to see him translating the symbols running from one guardian to the other.

"*ONLY BY SACRIFICE CAN THE TRUE GOLD BE FOUND.*

"*Only by sacrifice. . .*" Erskine muttered. He walked over to Luis and gestured to him to hand over the gun.

Ben saw Yara look at him in alarm, while all the colour drained from Raffie's face.

Luis raised his eyebrows, but handed over the weapon just the same.

Erskine swung the gun at the children, aiming it first at one and then at the other.

The muzzle came to rest pointing right at Yara.

"Local blood," Erskine said, matter-of-factly. "It would be a suitable sacrifice."

Raffie gasped. Yara stood very still and straight, her fists clenched by her sides.

*A blood sacrifice.* Ben gaped. Was that what Erskine thought he needed?

*There has to be some other way!*

But from the look on the Professor's face, there was no doubt about his intentions. Ben gave a shout and rushed at Erskine. Adrenaline drove him towards the gun – but suddenly his legs were kicked from under him, and he slammed on to his back, whacking his head.

Luis added a swift kick to Ben's ribs. "Keep out of it, Jaguar Boy," he growled.

Ben lay there, fighting the feeling of passing out. The outstretched arm of the guardian loomed over him. Through blurred vision he saw the upturned hand.

As he desperately tried to get to his feet, a thought came to him – something the shaman had said – what were the words again? *The way to El Dorado is. . .*

Ben fought to think clearly. He heard Rafael's frightened Portuguese; the sinister click as the gun was cocked. He saw Erskine's finger hover over the trigger. . .

"Don't shoot!" Ben managed to sit up. "I've worked it out! Stop!"

"Listen to the boy," Luis told Erskine, and the professor lowered the gun a little, looking curiously at Ben.

*Am I right?* Ben couldn't be sure. With a grunt he stood and reached for the hand of the guardian.

But the hand was too high. He tried to climb, but there were no footholds on the stonework.

He suddenly felt Yara and Rafael close, one each side of him.

"*The way to El Dorado is in the hands of the ancestors*," he whispered to them as they hoisted him on to their shoulders.

Ben came level with the guardian's upturned palm. And

that was when he saw them: carved into the hand, three grooves of different shapes. Wired with excitement, he quickly searched his pocket for the three gold icons.

He glanced down and saw Erskine watching him, the gun still pointed at Yara, the jaguar teeth making little bloody scratches in the man's forehead.

Ben took out the bat. Sunlight gleamed off the gold as he tried to fit it into one of the depressions; he breathed out with a smile as it clicked smoothly into place. "It's working!" he called down, and he saw Erskine smiling, craning to see.

Ben slotted in the gold bird, then held the monkey over the final groove and pressed it home. He felt the faintest of vibrations through the air, as if something invisible was close by, moving ghostlike, through the air. Pain throbbed through his arm and he eased himself from Yara and Rafael's shoulders and landed on the ground.

There was silence. A deep, harsh silence, as if time itself had stopped and turned to stone.

Ben waited, his breath catching. The silent stillness continued. There wasn't even a breath of wind.

But nothing happened.

"Nothing?" said Rafael in dismay. "How can it not have worked?"

Ben saw the smile fade from Erskine's face, and a muscle in his jaw twitch with irritation. The man raised the rifle at Yara again, his finger back on the trigger.

Rafael's rapid pleading cut through the silence: "Don't shoot her! Don't shoot!"

Without thinking, Ben sprang towards Erskine. He got between Yara and the gun. . . Stumbled. Fell. He heard Yara's cry of fear.

Then a crack like a gunshot ripped through the air.

# 21
# JOURNEY'S END

*"On the summit of the pass through the mountain, we came to a halt."*

MANUSCRIPT 512

The noise vibrated painfully through Ben's skull. He heard Raffie's shocked wail. Ben twisted his body, desperately trying to get back to his feet.

All he could think of was Yara.

*Yara. . .*

He felt someone crouched by him as he struggled to sit, someone helping him to get up.

*Yara?*

Ben gripped her arm, feeling a flood of relief. He frowned with confusion. "But I thought. . ."

"You were ready to sacrifice yourself for me." Her voice

was hoarse, hardly more than a whisper. She gestured past him at the rock face, unable to get out any more words.

Ben saw Erskine standing there with the rifle lowered; Luis with his mouth gaping. Raffie came close to Ben's shoulder as he turned, and the three children pressed together, staring at the rock face; at what had made the noise.

Where before there had been a smooth cliff, now there was a thin crack in the rock, spreading upwards like a break through ice.

The ground trembled, and the friends crouched, holding on to one another for support. The fissure widened. Loose chunks of rock tumbled from the splitting rock, and they stumbled back. There was a tremendous grating and scraping. The sound sent shock waves through Ben's whole body, and he saw Raffie clamp his hands over his ears, Yara's face crease up in pain.

Then, as quickly as it had started, the noise stopped. The crack had become wide enough to pass through – with a strange grey daylight showing beyond.

A flurry of emotion made Ben's knees tremble. The doorway to El Dorado was open. *The way is open!*

Erskine thrust the rifle back at Luis, then pushed Ben. "Go first!" he ordered.

Ben took a step, but Luis slipped forward to block the gap.

"Get out of the way!" Erskine's voice was spiky with irritation. "Jaguar Boy must lead us!"

Luis barred the way with the gun. Sweat patches stained his shirt. His scraggy face was grim and determined.

*This doesn't look good.* Ben edged back, his eyes gesturing to Yara and Raffie to do the same.

Erskine ploughed forward – only to be knocked to the ground by Luis. In one smooth movement, the hunter hoisted the rifle up and trained it on the professor. "I've been taking orders from you long enough, old man." Luis's voice was thick with hate. "Only two of us are going in there, *Prof.*" His eyes flicked towards Ben. "Just me and him."

"Luis. . ." Erskine opened his hands in a pacifying gesture as he slowly got back to his feet. He took a step towards Luis – but in an instant the hunter rotated the gun and slammed Erskine in the face with the rifle butt, forcing him back.

"Think I'm bluffing, old man?" Luis twitched the rifle, pointing back down the gully. "Take the other two kids with you and keep walking."

Erskine dabbed blood off his head with a handkerchief. "I agree you need Ben," he said. "But what about the hieroglyphs?" He took a small, shaky step towards Luis. "I'm the only one among us who can read them. The gold will be impossible to find without first decoding the messages on El Dorado's ancient monuments."

Ben saw a shadow of doubt pass over Luis's face.

Erskine took another tiny step. The edge of the jaguar skin trailed along the ground, and Ben felt his body tense as he watched. "I concede that you can have half of everything we find," the Professor said. "I couldn't have done any of this without you."

Ben's skin crawled. The professor's reasonable voice

didn't match his cold eyes at all. He saw Erskine inch forward as Luis hesitated.

And that moment's hesitation was all it took.

Erskine sprang, knocking the rifle sideways. There was a blur of movement as he and Luis grappled for the gun, blocking the entrance.

Luis was younger, fitter, but Erskine had taken him by surprise – and the hunter had the heavy pack still on his back, which unbalanced him.

There was a shot like a thunderclap, and Ben jolted with the noise. A red spray spattered the ground. Luis's eyes had grown wide as if in surprise. Ben heard his rasping breathing. A trickle of blood oozed out of the corner of the hunter's mouth. Then he was crumpling, gripping on to Ben as he fell.

Ben shrank back. He felt bile in his throat as Luis twitched and grasped. Then the hunter went still, a dark stain spreading under him, and little pools of blood collecting between the stones.

Erskine cradled the rifle a moment, then turned to Ben. "Now," he said. "Go through. Time is against us."

Ben numbly led the way, followed by a shaking Yara, then a stumbling Raffie. He stepped over the body straddling the entrance, trying not to look at the blood; the mess of chest.

A thought came to him. When Luis had kicked him to the ground, might he have been doing that to save him from getting shot?

Ben's shoulders scraped the rock as he went through

the narrow space. Inside, the air was strangely humid, and black ferns grew from alcoves in the stone. He pushed between the fronds, squeezing on and through and out. . .

Ben gazed at the scene beyond, his breath catching. He was at the top of a track that looped into a deep valley of rock – a stretched basin of rock, sealed at both ends.

And on the dry valley floor he could see buildings. Buildings! Houses of bare stone with slits for windows, and triangular ends where the roofs had once been. There was no sign of any movement. Broad, empty streets led to a huge central plaza.

And in the middle of the plaza was. . .

For a moment, Ben forgot about Erskine standing behind him with a gun; he even briefly forgot about the murder of Luis. His heart quivered.

Even from a distance, Ben knew without a doubt that he was looking at the temple. It dwarfed all the other buildings.

It was a kind of pyramid. Great blocks of grey stone were tiered into wide steps on each of its four sides. A steep ramp led to a box-shaped chamber at the top, with a gaping square doorway full of deep shadows.

*That's where I have to go.*

Yara squeezed Ben's arm, and his jaguar marks hurt from the pressure.

"El Dorado," breathed Rafael. He rubbed behind his glasses. "Look there." He pointed at the far end of the valley. Ben saw a towering, curving dam, and behind it he glimpsed the surface of a vast lake.

"Ingenious," Erskine muttered. "A freshwater reservoir. Vital in such an arid place. . . Now move!" He jabbed the gun barrel into Ben's back.

Ben started down the slope. He had to get to the temple fast. The brittle wings of a yellow moth disintegrated under his foot as he picked up his pace. There were only a couple of hours of daylight left at most. Somehow, he had to find the mask and keep it away from Erskine. Return it to the statue of the golden king.

He had to free the spirits, and hope Dad could then leave their world.

*But would Dad be allowed to?*

Ben's heart seemed to fill his chest. Inside his pocket he heard the jade and amber stones tap together in their pouch.

Somewhere in that temple, the golden king was waiting; his final trial was waiting.

Ben's boots kicked up dust as he hurried on.

Whatever that trial was, he was ready to face it.

*Nightfall is coming soon.*
*The necklace of jaguar claws is round the shaman's throat.*
*Fangs scratch his face.*
*Blood drips.*

*Slowly, I feel my four feet pad the temple chamber.*
*I see the tall man dressed in white. Three others.*
*The boy.*

*But fate must be followed.*
*I can do nothing to help him now.*

# PART 3

# CITY OF Z

*"Thence, spread out before our eyes, we saw in the open plain greater spectacles for our vision of admiration and wonder . . . a great city."*

— MANUSCRIPT 512

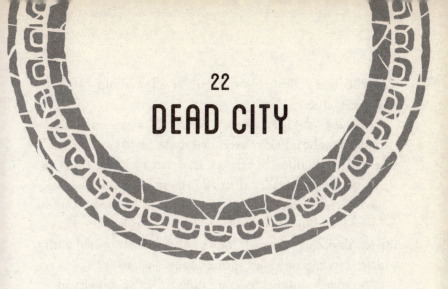

## 22
# DEAD CITY

*"We encountered no other road except the one that led to the dead city."*

MANUSCRIPT 512

Ben hurried down the slope in the fading light. El Dorado stretched below, eerily silent, the temple at its centre.

"Faster!" Erskine hissed, gesturing with the rifle.

Ben kept alert, exchanging stolen glances with Yara and Rafael, looking for a chance – any chance – to get the gun off Erskine; to escape.

Mist brushed Ben's face like ghostly fingertips. The valley walls rose round them. Clouds swirled above, looking out of place over such a parched landscape.

"There must be funny weather here," whispered Rafael.

"Maybe that's why this City never showed up on any satellite pictures."

*Has that kept El Dorado secret all these years?* Ben wondered as he quickly descended the series of switchbacks. He had the sudden, ominous sensation of being trapped here, between the valley cliffs and the swirling sky.

As they reached the bottom, the track levelled off and widened, and in front of Ben towered a marble archway. As he led the others through, he saw that it was covered with ornate carvings of water: springs, fountains, rivers.

"Strange," commented Yara quietly. "In such a dry, dry place."

Ben followed the paved street, peering into the low doorways of the stone houses. He scanned round for any signs of movement, but there was nothing – only the dark windows staring back at him, like empty eyes.

"Not much of a city of gold," muttered Rafael. He poked his head through a doorway carved round with crumbling hieroglyphs.

Ben saw brightly coloured glass beads scattered around the entrance – from a necklace perhaps, the string long since decayed away. He saw Yara pick up a small stone carving of a mother, arms wrapped round her child.

"Keep walking!" Erskine wrenched Yara's arm so that she dropped the figure. "All of you!"

Ben continued on. *How long since anybody walked this street?* he wondered. He looked at the grey flagstones polished smooth by centuries of footsteps. A breeze rippled the fabric of his shirt, and for a moment he heard the muted sounds of talk, shouts, laughter.

Then there was just the wind sighing through gaps in the stonework and the rushed tread of their feet. His marks throbbed even more than when he'd seen the black jaguar dead. *Who had lived here? Why had they left?*

The temple loomed up ahead.

"Faster!" Erskine pulled Rafael roughly forward.

Yara moved ahead of Ben – but Erskine yanked her back by the hair.

"Jaguar Boy must always go first." He clamped her chin in his fist. "He was chosen for this. Clear?"

Ben moved to pull him away from her, but a punch slammed his cheek and he fell to the ground.

Erskine stood over him. Ben looked at the empty eye sockets of the jaguar's head on Erskine's scalp, and the bloody fangs resting against his forehead.

Ben's jaw tensed as he got to his feet. Whatever happened, Erskine was never going to put on the golden king's mask.

*I am going to stop you.*

But Ben knew he had to hurry. Through the veil of cloud the light was dimming fast.

He came out into the plaza and stumbled a little as he stared at the temple dominating its centre. Its great grey steps rose upwards until it seemed to fill the whole sky. Even from a distance it had looked imposing, but close up was something else entirely.

Ben gazed at the huge, smooth blocks that made up its

stepped sides. His eyes followed the steep ramp to the dark doorway at the top.

"Careful in there," Rafael panted from close behind, as Ben started up the incline. "The Ancients will have definitely booby-trapped this place!"

"We have got to get rid of the gun!" hissed Yara. "We cannot let Erskine take the mask!"

"Be ready," Ben mouthed back. He'd have to make a move soon.

Very soon.

Up they climbed, Ben's leg muscles tensed against the gradient, his stomach lurching from the dizzying drop as he got higher.

They arrived at the top, panting, Ben's nerves taut with expectation.

"Go inside" Erskine ordered.

With a wary nod to his friends, Ben passed first through the square entrance into the deep shadows beyond.

A passageway disappeared into the gloom. Pale beams came from high openings, picking out animal-like faces carved along the walls. The eyes seemed to watch Ben as he walked past them, and the further along the corridor he went, the more sinister the faces became in the decreased light – the teeth sharper, the eyes like holes.

"Hurry!" Erskine swung the rifle in irritation. He had a wild look that made Ben's skin shudder.

The passageway ended, and Ben came to a stop in front of a high stone door.

The professor peered at the hieroglyphs carved there in

the half-light. "A message from the Ancients," he muttered, frowning. "Some kind of warning. . . A curse."

Ben's throat tightened. *Curse?*

"*Choose freely. . .*" Erskine translated. "*But beware.*"

"*CHOOSE FREELY, BUT BEWARE,*
*FOR ONLY ONE WILL BE*
*THE GOLDEN KING'S TRUE FACE.*
*THE KING WILL PROTECT HIS CITY*
*FROM THOSE NOT PURE IN HEART,*
*FROM HE WHO CHOOSES FALSE.*"

"Go through!" Erskine barked.

Ben turned to look at Yara and Rafael, seeing their eyes wide in the murky light. Heart hammering, he pressed his hands on the door and heaved it open – then blinked as light spilled over him and he stepped forward into it.

He was in a three-sided chamber, where there was an opening stretching right down to the floor – a wide window that hadn't been visible from the top of the track. It gave a view right down the valley, across the houses and towards the dam.

"At last," he heard Erskine whisper. He saw the professor lit by a strange gold sheen as light was reflected on to him by something in the room.

And as Ben's eyes adjusted, he saw it – in the dead centre of the room – on a high plinth made up of polished black marble steps. He hardly heard Raffie's excited cries, or Yara's murmurs of amazement. He couldn't take his gaze away from the gold statue on top of the plinth.

The statue was taller than a real man, and not really a man at all. The feet were paws; and instead of fingers, the raised hands were edged with razor-sharp claws. A sweeping tail curved from behind.

*The golden king.*

Ben edged nearer. He felt the jaguar marks burn with some kind of intense energy, at once painful and thrilling.

"Look at the head." Yara pressed close against Ben's shoulder, and he felt her tremble. "He has no face!"

Ben stared up at the featureless gold surface where the face should have been. It was a haunting sight.

"Ben!" Rafael pointed a shaky finger.

Lying on the black marble of the bottom step, Ben saw two masks.

Two identical gold masks.

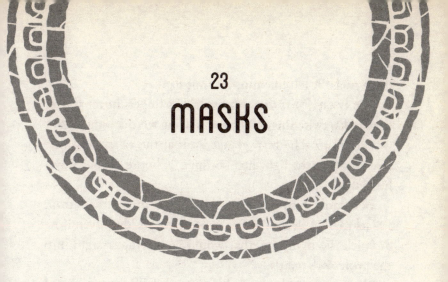

# 23
# MASKS

Two ornate gold masks, each decorated more beautifully than anything Ben had ever seen. Not even the bat or bird or monkey icons could match them.

To Ben, the masks looked exactly the same, with gaping jaws and sleek, bared fangs; delicately curling whiskers and almond-shaped eye sockets.

Everything about the masks spoke of beauty, strength, power.

A jaguar. Two jaguars.

"Awesome," breathed Yara.

Rafael looked at Ben in panic mode. "How are you going to know which is the golden king's true face? Remember the curse on the door? If you choose the wrong one, you are bound to die a horrible and painful death!"

"You have to be sure, Ben," Yara agreed. "This must be the final trial our legend speaks of."

*My final trial.*

How long had it been since Ben had first started out on

these trials? It felt like months, not days.

"Only one," Erskine muttered. His fingers hovered over the masks, twitching, as if he was dying to touch them, but was afraid to. The man glanced out at the valley, and Ben saw how pale the light had become. "Choose, Jaguar Boy!" he snarled.

Ben looked from one mask to the other, then from Rafael to Yara, feeling panic squeeze his insides. Even if he *did* pick the right one, that would be playing straight into the professor's hands.

"I must wear the mask before nightfall!" Erskine lifted the gun and held the barrel to Rafael's head. "*Choose!*"

"Wait!" *There must be a way to know*, Ben told himself desperately.

He looked from one to the other, trying to detect any differences between them. The weak light created a sheen across the masks, drawing him closer. But he was hesitant to actually touch them. He peered closely at the left one, seeing his worried face reflected in the smoother parts of its gold surface.

Ben focused on the other mask. Was there anything about the design that might single it out? No, both seemed identical in every way.

Did one have a different *feeling* compared to the other?

"Choose." Erskine's voice cut acrosss Ben's thinking, low and dangerous. He saw the man tap Rafael's head with the tip of the gun, and Raffie lifted his chin and closed his eyes, his face deathly pale.

Ben looked at the second mask again in frustration.

There had to be *something*; some way to tell which one was the true mask!

He peered closer at them, scanning their surfaces – then felt a small jolt go through him.

Ben looked again, at the right mask, then at the left one, trying to take in what he was seeing.

The mask on the left was as it had been when he'd first scrutinized it, reflecting back Ben's face in its smooth parts.

But it was the mask on the right that really caught his attention.

For reflected in the gold of that right-hand mask wasn't Ben's face at all. Instead, blinking back at him, was the face of a jaguar. *His jaguar!*

Their eyes locked – Ben and the jaguar – as they had done that day on the boat. Emotion surged through Ben. This mask was the one – it must be! *The golden king's true face!*

Ben had the urge to shout what he'd seen to the others, but he forced himself to show zero emotion. Instead, he continued to look at the masks, as if still deciding. It was now or never time with Erskine. Or Dad was never coming back.

And the plan he was formulating in his head was going to be risky. Too risky.

*But I have to try.*

Ben stared steadily at Yara, flicking his eyes towards Raffie, then back at her – *Be ready* – and saw the tiniest worried nod in reply.

"Choose *now*!" He saw Erskine his finger tense against

the trigger.

"Don't shoot!" said Ben quickly. "I know which it is."

"Don't tell him, Ben!" cried Rafael in anguish. His forehead was beaded with sweat. "What about your dad? You'll never save him if Erskine gets the mask!

Ben shook his head. "We've lost, Rafael," he said, letting his body sag. "We don't even know if Dad *can* come back." Pulse racing, he held one of the masks out to Erskine, and saw the rifle lower a little.

Erskine narrowed his eyes, then reached to take it.

And it was in that split second, while Erskine's attention was fixed on being given the mask, that Ben made his move.

He flung the mask towards Erskine, taking him completely off guard, then knocked the rifle away with a cry.

The gun clattered to the floor, going off with a deafening crack. Shards of black marble sprayed across the floor as the bullet hit the plinth. Ben sprang to take the other mask.

Out of the corner of his eye, Ben saw Rafael lurch back from the blast. He went down hard on to the stone flags and lay there, holding his head.

"*Go*, Ben!" screamed Yara. With a yell, she kicked the gun away and it clattered over the stone paving, sliding through the opening and dropping out of sight. With a roar, Erskine swivelled to land a punch on Yara's side, and she spun back with a clipped shout.

"*Yara! Raffie!*" Ben saw Erskine hurtling towards him – but he couldn't seem to move. His friends. . . They needed help. . .

"You must complete your trials, Ben!" Yara cried from

the floor, clutching her leg. "Leave us! Go!"

Ben came to his senses and leapt up the first marble step of the statue's plinth, only a few seconds ahead of Erskine. He jumped on to the next step, and then the next, scrabbling to find grip on the polished surface, struggling to keep hold of the heavy mask.

He got to the top step, reaching the paw feet of the king, and used both hands to lift the mask towards the empty face.

Brushing against the gold statue sent shock waves through Ben's body as he stretched, and he felt his jaguar marks go hot, as if a branding iron had been pressed on to his bare skin.

He saw Erskine scaling the plinth, coming after him, and Ben gulped air as he forced himself to fight the pain, and reach higher. *Higher!*

There were only minutes of daylight left. Only seconds before he reached his goal.

# 24
# THE ONE

Ben put on a burst of speed, but Erskine was gaining. Rather than slow him, the jaguar pelt seemed to give the man extra strength.

As Ben lifted the mask level with the statue's head, he suddenly felt a tight grip on his boot. He jerked his leg savagely, again and again, finally managing to pull his foot away – then kicked down hard with it, making contact with Erskine's jaw. Glancing down, Ben saw him thrown off balance and nearly fall from the plinth.

The move bought Ben a few precious seconds. He clasped the mask in two hands and hoisted it towards the empty face, stretching up, desperate to find the crucial extra height he needed.

Thoughts came to him in snatches as he strained upwards: *When the mask is replaced . . . his power will be restored . . . he will welcome all lost spirits into the sanctuary of his city. . .*

*This is it!* Ben told himself. *Just a little higher!* With a cry of effort, he lifted the mask level with the head, and he felt a strong pull between the two surfaces, as if they were being drawn together by some strange magnetic force.

"*Dad*," Ben whispered. He fixed the mask into place, and it fitted exactly against the curving face, clamping smoothly round it.

He heard Erskine give a shout – and watched him slither down the statue.

Ben drew back and held his breath, hardly believing what he'd done, hardly daring to hope. He waited, watching.

The seconds ticked by. . . His eyes flicked at his friends, and he saw Yara crawl towards Rafael and help him to sit up, and the two of them gazed up at Ben with questioning looks.

Panic squeezed Ben's chest. What was wrong? Had the mask not attached properly? He reached up again to check. It was locked rigidly in place, but still Ben had no feeling of any kind of change.

*Where are the spirits? I should feel something, surely*, Ben thought – *something* has to happen.

But the gold was cold under his touch. Dead.

The mask's lustre faded in the diminishing light, its intricate patterns disappearing into shadow.

"It hasn't worked?" Erskine stared up at the statue, his lips curling into a small smile. "It hasn't worked."

"It has to," gasped Ben. His mind buzzed with confusion. Had he been too late? But there was still light outside – it wasn't nightfall yet.

Still the mask stared back at him, lifeless. Had the

reflection he'd seen been a trick?

Erskine scooped the other mask from the floor. "You failed, Jaguar Boy."

He strode towards the window.

Ben kept his position on the plinth, watching the professor.

"You chose the wrong mask, Ben?" Yara chewed her lip.

"How did you decide which one to take?" fretted Rafael.

"I'm sure I *did* choose the right one," Ben told them. He watched Erskine angle the mask in his hands, using the light from the window opening to examine it; then the professor lifted it to his face.

The jaguar pelt bristled round the man's shoulders. Ben saw Luis's dried blood on Erskine's hands as he held the gold mask.

*Gold and blood.*

Ben's mind snapped back to his visions and what they had shown him; the sufferings of the past, all because of gold: the destruction of sacred objects; the disease; the murders. The unquiet spirits needed a sanctuary, he believed that more than ever now.

And he needed his dad back.

"I *did* choose the true mask, Yara," Ben said again, hearing the sureness in his voice. "You've got the wrong one, Erskine."

"You would say that, Jaguar Boy!" the professor scoffed. "Anything to deceive me!"

And without another word, with a sweeping gesture, Erskine put the mask on.

Ben cried out. He heard Yara and Rafael gasp. All three

of them stared at Erskine standing by the chamber opening. The thick, dark fur was spread wide over his shoulders and hung down in a great wave. The jaguar's fangs over Erskine's head touched the top surface of the gold.

The man seemed taller, broader, thought Ben with a shudder. Through the mask, the man's cold eyes were looking straight at Ben.

Yara spoke up. "There is something happening!"

Ben craned forward, trying to make out what was going on. He saw a movement at the border of the mask. It was as if something alive was scuttling over the surface, making the metal flex and ripple.

Tendrils of gold were growing out of the edges, flicking backwards and forwards, searching for skin to latch on to. When they found flesh, their ends attached, then swelled, sealing the mask on to Erskine's face.

The professor's mouth broke into a small smile, and his chest expanded as he drew in a deep breath.

"No!" Yara's face was tight with panic.

"It's working, Ben," Rafael wailed up at him.

Ben gaped at the Professor, fascinated and horrified at the same time as the gold tendrils continued to spread. They slithered down Erskine's neck, finding the gap along the collar of his shirt. The man's eyes widened. His smile vanished. A choking sound bubbled from his throat.

And now Erskine's hands were on the mask, wrenching at it, trying to prise it off.

# 25
# THE GOLDEN MAN

Erskine tore at the mask, but it was fixed solidly to his face, the gold flooding over and into his skin, merging with his body.

Ben saw him wrestle the jaguar pelt from his back and it fell to the floor, but that did nothing to stop what was happening.

Erskine's shoulders went rigid. His flailing arms became restricted to jerky, desperate swipes. Now he seemed able to move his arms only from the elbow, no longer able to reach the mask. Then his arms locked in a contorted, pleading gesture. His hands grasped at the air.

"What's happening?" cried Rafael.

Ben saw a yellow colour appear from the sleeves of Erskine's jacket, staining the skin as it moved over the backs of his hands, then his palms, then crawled along his fingers. The professor's fingertips twitched and then went still, fixed into stiff claws.

Yara gave a horrified cry. "He is turning to gold!"

Screams of agony echoed round the chamber and Ben had a sickening image of the gold seeking out living tissue; seeping through skin, muscle, bone; burrowing deeper; reaching towards the lungs, the heart. . .

Then Erskine's shrieks were cut short. Through the mask Ben saw his mouth frozen open, a garish glow to his lips and teeth. Gold spread towards his scalp, turning even the shafts of hair to brittle strands of metal.

Only the man's legs were still able to move. He stumbled round the room, his steps rigid with the growing weight of his body.

Ben saw him dangerously close to the plummeting drop from the chamber, and instinctively he started forward to try to pull him back. . .

But it was too late. The man teetered on the edge, his legs locked, his eyes glazed over, the colour of sulphur. . .

And he fell.

There were the clangs of metal smashing against stone as the gold man hit the steep steps of the temple, and Ben winced with each thud, shuddering as the sounds faded into nothing.

And then the first earthquake hit.

# 26
# FLOOD

The temple chamber shook. A crack appeared in one wall, branching like a broken artery across the stonework.

"We've got to get out!" Ben shouted to his friends.

"But you have to complete your trials, Ben!" Yara cried, as she and Rafael crouched on the floor, eyes wide.

"But I don't know. . ." Ben's words were cut short as another quake struck. A zigzagging gap appeared in the floor. He felt the plinth lurch, and he shunted down on to the bottom step. A floor slab jutted up like a gravestone. All of them winced as a great chunk of masonry slammed down from the ceiling and shattered. Jagged rubble blocked the stone door.

"There's still some daylight left!" Rafael blinked at Ben through his glasses, only one shattered lens still in its frame.

"But I don't know what else to do!" Ben told them desperately.

The temple chamber rattled. There was the grating squeal of stone against stone. And over the noise of the earthquake came another even more menacing sound from the far end of the valley.

From his vantage point, Ben stared out through the chamber opening.

His eye skimmed over the buildings of El Dorado, along the valley; to the great stone barricade at the far end.

*The dam.*

Cracks had appeared in its surface and water was pouring through, quickly becoming torrents as the barrier fragmented.

Another tremor hit, and with an explosive thud, the dam gave way. Water burst out, gushing in a great, dark wave towards the city; a gigantic wall of water swallowing everything in its path. The earthquakes died away, but the water was unstoppable. It cascaded from the broken dam and raced along the streets, submerging whole houses within seconds.

For a few moments Ben stayed there frozen, watching the wave approach. By the time he uttered a warning shout, it was already way too late.

Water smashed against the great temple and slammed across the floor, swirling up to flood the chamber.

Ben gasped as a shock of cold spilled into his boots, and up his legs to his hips.

"Can't swim!" Rafael's arms flailed, one eye huge through the broken lens as the current lifted him off the floor.

"*Raffie!*"

Seeing Yara kick towards Raffie and clamp an arm under his chin, Ben braced himself to dive from the statue and go to them, but she shook her head hard at him.

"The mask!" Ben could hardly hear her shout over the hiss of currents. Yara was mouthing something else now, as she trod water, pointing wildly at the statue as she fought to keep herself and Rafael afloat, but Ben couldn't make out what she was saying.

Water rose up Ben's chest, the cold of it making him short of breath, and he hoisted himself up on to the top step of the plinth. He scanned the flooding statue of the golden king, then the swamped chamber.

The light was almost gone. Shadows reached towards him. The black jaguar skin was being carried on the water. Ben remembered the reflection of the jaguar's face he'd seen in the mask.

The floating skin rotated fast so that the lifeless head looked away, then faced Ben, then looked away again, the empty sockets seeming so unnatural without. . .

Ben straightened, gasping. It was suddenly so clear. *Of course. Of course!*

Yara must have read the look on Ben's face, because there was new grim excitement in her own strained features. He saw her nod hard.

More water poured in with renewed ferocity, and Ben got unsteadily to his feet as this new burst washed over the top of the plinth, rising rapidly. He felt the dead weight of his saturated clothes as the level reached his throat.

*You can do this*, he told himself. *You were chosen for this.*

As the last light disappeared from the chamber, Ben ran his fingers up the statue's neck, clutching at the gold, feeling for the face.

Battling the tug of water, he pulled the sodden bark pouch from his pocket, and lifted it clear of the surface. He extracted the jade and amber spheres from inside.

They felt warm under his touch as Ben gripped them hard and raised them towards the face of the golden king. He held his breath as water streamed over his mouth and nose.

*Free the spirits*, he pleaded silently. *Give them sanctuary here.*

*Please allow my dad to leave their world.*

He slotted the stones into the eye sockets of the mask, seeing them fuse seamlessly into place.

The spheres glistened with a soft luminescence as they were covered with water.

Ben let go, heart thudding, and began to drift away. From under the water he saw a glow ripple over the mask, warmth radiating as its gold merged with the gold of the statue. The glow spread downwards through the water, until the whole of the golden king – the whole chamber – shone with a pulsing light.

Yara and Rafael's faces glowed gold. Ben swam to them and they clung together as they were swept from the chamber into deep, open water.

Ben stared round them as he trod water beside Yara, with Rafael in between.

Where the valley had once been there was now a vast lake, from which only the very top stones of the temple could be seen. Round it the water had an otherworldly glow. The sky was now strangely cloudless; a rust-coloured moon was rising over the lip of its sheer sides, casting ghostly beams.

None of the three friends spoke. They let the fast-rising currents carry them, transporting them into the heart of the lake.

*Where are the unquiet spirits?* thought Ben. *Where's Dad?*

Ben's numb fingers gripped Rafael. He felt the water pressed round, draining away his body heat; slowing down his senses. *How long can we float like this, in such cold water?*

He thought of trying to swim towards the sheer rock edge of the basin, but his legs just wouldn't respond, his aching muscles seizing up. He was exhausted, struggling to keep himself afloat now, let alone Rafael as well, and he could see Yara was having the same difficulties. In the night sky, Ben saw the first star appear, and then another. More stars emerged, until the night sky was teeming with them, their points reflected in the dark water.

The final, uppermost part of the temple submerged, and El Dorado was gone, hidden beneath the expanse of rippling lights.

Ben felt himself start to sink.

And then they came. . .

# 27
# REDEMPTION

*"and in the ruined hall are seen works of beauty"*

MANUSCRIPT 512

There was a sighing, like a long, slow breath out. It was nothing more than a vague sensation to Ben at first, a faint shimmer in the water around him like a heat haze.

Then something was moving through the water towards them. Flitting shapes that seemed to be all at once both liquid and light.

Now Ben could make out ghostly figures, and they were heading directly at them, nearer by the second. He clung to Rafael and saw Yara's eyes wide with fear.

Ben cried out as the first of the eerie forms reached him in a wave, passing by him, through him. . . The sensation was like a pulse of electricity; like rushing bubbles of oxygen across his skin. Warming.

Women, men, children. . . streaming past and through, part of the water, and yet separate from it. Their fluid fingertips brushed Ben. He heard their laughter, strung like coloured beads along the threads of current. He saw that their eyes were wide with anticipation.

Ben felt Rafael tense, and then relax, held up by the water, his face brimming with wonder. Yara's eyes shone.

Around them became thick with the spirits, and now there were faces Ben recognized.

They were the people from his visions – the boy with the long, dark hair, the shoals of golden fish of his bracelet glimmering on his arm as he came close.

There was the little girl with the round face, her skin no longer marked with disease, her features lit by an unearthly glow.

There was the mother with her baby, her expression serene; her child sleeping contentedly in her arms.

Smiling, the spirits reached out to touch Ben as they passed, and all around him the water seemed alive with them.

They circled, stretched out their arms in greeting, and in farewell. Ben tried to clutch their hands, but it was impossible to get a hold. They slipped through his fingers like air, like smoke, and continued on.

Still they came, those released spirits: the people of the forests, the conquistadors, the lost explorers, until it seemed to Ben that there was no water at all, only their shifting, flowing forms. They moved across the water, and then, with barely a ripple, dived towards their sanctuary; spiralling into the secret depths of El Dorado.

Ben looked urgently into the spirits' swirling faces, searching, hoping. . .

And finally he saw what he had been yearning to see.

There was a figure being carried fast towards him with the spirits.

*Dad.*

A longing shivered through Ben as he reached out towards his father.

But he was coming so quickly – would he be able to catch hold of him; to stop him from continuing on with the spirits, away and down? Ben stretched through the water, desperately straining against the current.

*Give him back to me.* . . "Please give my dad back!" He shouted out the words.

As the spirits skimmed past, Ben snatched at Dad's arm, gasping as he felt real fabric, real flesh. *Dad is alive!* Ben held on as tight as he could, but already he could feel his grasp slipping.

"No!" Ben tried to increase his grip, but dad's momentum was too strong. And just as dad was about to spin away from him, Rafael and Yara shot out their arms, so that all three children had a hold.

*Live*, voices whispered through the water. *Live!*

And the four of them drifted away from the river of spirits, clutching one another.

The water level rose still higher, and they were pushed up the side of the valley as it continued to fill, pulling them to the very top of the basin.

There was no time to feel afraid.

They clasped hands tight, fingers interlocking as the water overspilled the rim of rock. And they were swept over and down. . .

Down.

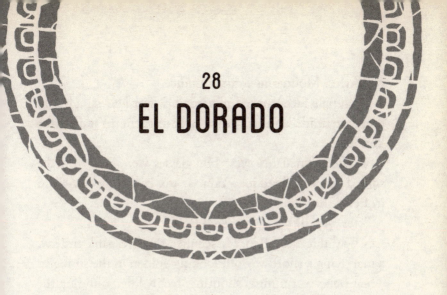

# 28
# EL DORADO

*"Shadow," said he,*
*"Where can it be—*
*This land of Eldorado?"*

EDGAR ALLEN POE (1809—1849)

Ben felt the sun on his back. A gritty taste on his tongue. From somewhere nearby came the sound of moving water.

What had happened came back to him in snatches. Being carried over and down, riding the great smooth water in the darkness, like he had been on the back of some black living creature.

*Dad? Yara? Raffie?*

He dug his fingers into sand and levered himself up, getting shakily to his feet, and his eyes adjusting to the scene: a sluggish river; a rocky ridge on one side, covered with trees. Mountains in the distance.

Two pale faces turned towards his, wet hair clinging to their foreheads, and he rushed over to them. "Yara! Raffie! You OK?"

Raffie opened his eyes. His glasses were gone, but he smiled in Ben's direction. Yara sat up, coughing. "You did it, Ben," she said.

"Yes, you did it!" whispered Rafael.

"*We* did it," said Ben. He scanned the riverbank and saw a man lying a short way off, looking golden in the sunlight. Then Ben was running, shouting, feet wildly pounding the shore. He sank to his knees and cradled his dad's head in his hands.

Dad looked up at him, eyes glinting. "Told you I'd find you, Ben," he joked.

Ben smiled back, nodding.

Dad sat up as Yara guided Rafael over. "Raffie! You're all right! Your dad will be so relieved!" He pulled him into a hug and Raffie beamed, tears running down his cheeks.

"This is Yara," said Ben.

Dad shook her hand and she flung her arms around his neck, making him laugh out loud.

"Got your ring." Ben slipped it off his thumb and handed it over, and Dad gripped it in his fist, lips tight.

"Thanks, son," he managed at last.

They all sat huddled on the bank for a while in silence, gathering their strength, then telling each other their stories. . .

Sunbursts sparkled on the river. Ben remembered the

faces he'd looked into. Their joy at their finally finding peace; at their finding a home.

Ben's mind still bubbled with questions. "So now it's your turn to tell us, Dad – what happened to you?"

Dad ran his fingers through his wet hair. "Well . . . I remember jumping from the boat; getting swept down the rapids."

"Yes, how on earth did you survive *that*?" exclaimed Rafael with bewilderment. "It was bad enough by canoe!"

Dad rubbed his forehead. " Funny thing is, I don't think I did! I mean, I think I must have drowned, but – now this is going to sound totally nutty – but, I was somehow also still alive."

"But what did that feel like?" Ben asked. "And where were you all this time?"

"I really don't know where I was," Dad said. "How can I describe it? It was kind of like being asleep under water, but never being able to wake up."

"That makes sense," said Yara. "My grandfather always taught me that the Drowned Ghosts rapids are a doorway to the spirit world."

"I dreamt of you, Ben," Dad said, squeezing his arm. "I saw snatches of what was happening to you, I think."

"I was wondering," Rafael said, "about when Professor Erskine wore the wrong mask. According to me, it was his own greed for gold that killed him in the end – remember the warning on the chamber door? *The king will protect his city from he who chooses false.* That's why he was turned to gold."

"And why the earthquakes started," added Yara. "To trigger the flood and hide El Dorado under a protective lake." She grinned. "How awesome was that!"

Dad ruffled Ben's hair. "Well, El Dorado might be lost again, but you three found it," he said quietly. "Didn't you?" He gave a long, slow whistle; a hoarse little laugh.

Ben gripped his arm. "But we can never tell anyone, Dad! It's the only safe place the spirits have left, and if people find out. . ."

"'Course we won't tell," reassured Dad. "Who would believe us anyway?"

"You can't even tell your dad, Raffie," warned Yara. "We all have to promise!"

"Especially my father!" said Rafael. "But I tell you something – Pa won't be telling me to toughen up after this adventure, that's for sure!"

"Good one, Raffie!" Ben punched him playfully on the arm.

"Ow!"

The indignant look on Rafael's face made them all burst out laughing, even Raffie himself, and then the four of them grasped hands and made the promise.

Ben let go of his dad's hand and gazed out towards the mountains. "Will El Dorado ever be found again, do you think?"

Dad smiled, a thoughtful smile. "Maybe. People will always be searching for their El Dorados, won't they?"

"But what I still want to know," said Yara, "is where do you think my grandfather got the golden king's amber and jade spheres from in the first place?"

Ben shrugged. "Passed down from the Ancients through generations of shamans, maybe? Hey – look!" He pointed a finger in amazement. "You can go and ask him yourself!"

"Grandfather!" Yara let out a delighted shout and scrambled to her feet.

There, above them on the ridge, Ben saw a line of figures. The shaman and a group of people Ben recognized from Yara's village, making their way towards them.

"He found us!" Yara cried. "He must have spoken to the Ancestors!"

Looking at the line of villagers, Ben was reminded of the spirit faces he'd seen moving through the water, and for a moment it was like he was seeing a bridge, linking past and present.

As they got closer Ben saw the shaman hold his arms out to his granddaughter, his eyes alight. He was smiling so that his whole wise face broke into deep creases. Yelping with delight, Yara splashed across the river and into his arms.

And it was while everyone was talking and laughing and hugging that Ben saw it. Up high on the ridge where the shaman had just been standing.

One eye a burning amber, the other a deep jade green.

Their gazes locked, one last time.

Then the black jaguar was gone.

# ACKNOWLEDGEMENTS

Virginia Bianchini
Matt Dickinson
Colonel Percy Fawcett
Caterina Galatá
Jamie Gregory
Isabella Gustincich
Gen Herr
Caroline Johnson
Captain David Maybury
Sarah Mussi
Polly Phillips
Flight Commander Marco Zadnik